THE BEATING HEART

Translated By

Akula Gnana Dev
N.R. Thapaswy

From The Original Telugu Version Of
NUTHALAPATI NAGESWARA RAO

THE BEATING HEART
By
NUTHALAPATI NAGESWARA RAO

First Edition Aug-2023

ISBN (Paperback): 978-81-963835-4-1

Published By
Kasturi Vijayam,
3-50, Main Road,
Dokiparru Village -521322
Krishna Dist., Andhra Pradesh, India.

Book Available
@
Amazon, flipkart, Google Play, ebooks, Rakuten and KOBO

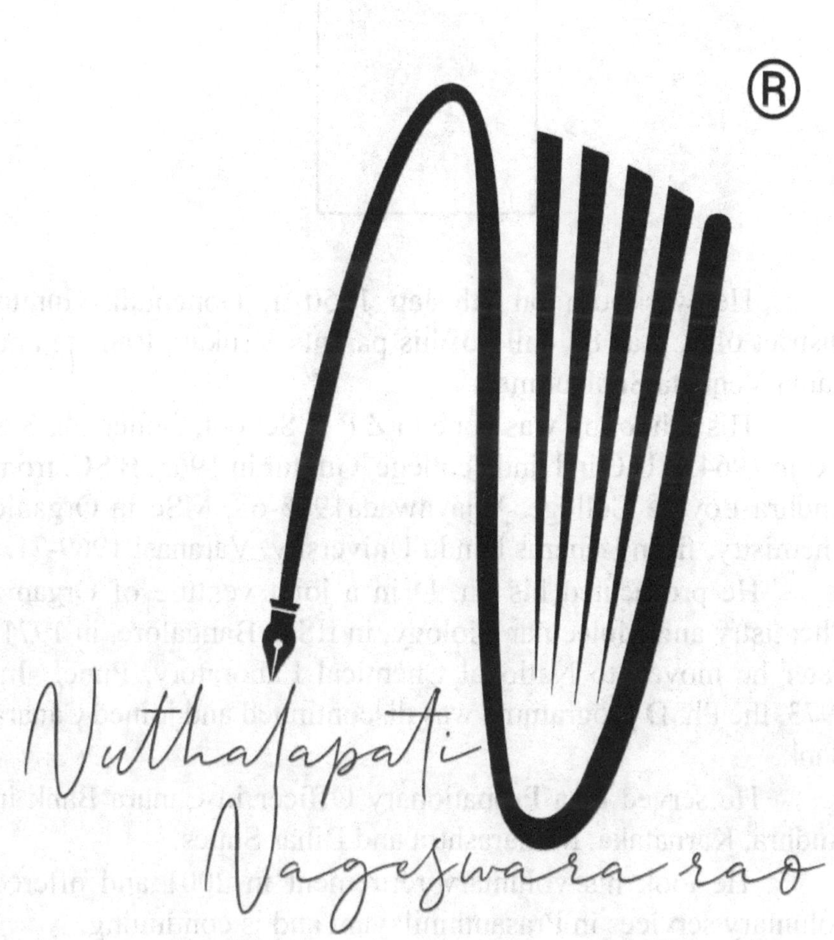

TM No. 5578002 / 23.8.2022

NNR WRITING HOUSE SINCE 1975

AKULA GNANA DEV

He was born on 4th Jan 1950 at Donepudi, Guntur District of A.P as 8th child of his parents Venkata Ratnam and Rama Venkata Subbamma.

His schooling was done in Z P H School, Donepudi, S S L C in 1964, P U C in Hindu college, Guntur in 1965. B SC, from Andhra Loyola College, Vijayawada1965-68, MSc in Organic Chemistry, from Banaras Hindu University, Varanasi 1969-71.

He prosecuted his Ph. D in a joint venture of Organic Chemistry and Molecular Biology, in IISC, Bangalore, in 1971. Later he moved to National Chemical Laboratory, Pune. In, 1973, the Ph. D programme was discontinued and joined Canara Bank.

He served as a Probationary Officer in Canara Bank in Andhra, Karnataka, Maharashtra and Bihar States.

He took his voluntary retirement in 2001 and offered voluntary services in Prasanthinilayam and is continuing.

N.R. Thapaswy

He was born on 17th April 1948 at GOVADA Village, Tenali taluk, Guntur Dt, A.P, as the third child of his parents 'Kavi Bhushan' N. Venkata Ratna Kavi, a self-sculpted scholar in Telugu, English and Sanskrit and N.Manga Devi a school teacher.

His elder sister Kolakaluri Swarupa Rani is a pioneer of Feminist Classical Poetry in Modern Telugu Literature.

He now lives at Chennai with his wife Smt. Deena. He is a free thinker.

PRELUDE
N.R. Thapaswy

Man is a thinking animal. Literature is the mirror in which society regards her face and rectifies the errors. A novel is a prose cinema, short story a snap shot.

Mr. N. Nageswara Rao, a self taught literary artist, who happened to already carve a niche for himself in Telugu literature with his publication of many works, herewith holds a Magic mirror to the joys and sorrows of middle class families.

In fact, this is the English rendition of his original Telugu collection of short stories entitled '*Kathala Kadambam*'.

In the opening story "Bond of Love", a loving mother who had undergone untold suffering for the brought up of his son is criminally neglected by him, in her oldage.

In another one, "Cadaver Tub", which can be fixed as the best story of his compilation, an arrogant son who hates his sacrificial father, all his life, at last, realises his greatness past his sad, demise, and repents.

In the same fashion, all the stories deliver some practical message or the other to the reader to elevate himself from what he is, to what he is to be.

I feel the writer has come out successful in his endeavor in creating such enchanting chiaroscuro of pragmatic life which will be a valuable addition to the library of a discerning Bibliophile!

My three cheers to my venerable friend 'Nag!' for his honouraficabilitudinity!

*

AUTHOR'S FEW WORDS

On the advice of some foreign Telugu literary friends, I tried to publish the English version of 'Kadhala Kadambam' which was published in Telugu as it would be easily accessible to the world readers and would gain popularity if translated into English language.

As a result, the stories should be brought in a volume and it will be convenient to the readers if they were available in book form. Mr. Akula Gnandev responded voluntarily with the idea that it would be better to translate the book in English language, hoping for a wider audience, as writing in Telugu language is limited to those who read and understand Telugu. Next, Mr. N. R Thapaswy, who gave a final shape in all respects of the content by spending his precious time, completed the translation into English with the Title "The Beating Heart".

It is gratifying that people appreciate that stories are the things that walk alive around us at every step of the way of life. I inform you that with your encouragement I will translate more works into English and bring them before you all.

I sincerely thanking to my friend Madhav, renowned cartoonist who expressed the feelings of the stories in the most beautiful way and to the artist Wilson D'souza who created my picture with colours from his brush, to the publisher of 'Kasturi Vijayam' who published the book in an attractive way for the readers and literature lovers at a very affordable price. Special thanks to my wife Chodavarapu Sudha Rani and my family members for their support and encouragement.

Feedback on this prestigious work may be submitted to the below noted email / WhatsApp for which I will be grateful.

Yours
Nuthalapati Nageswara Rao
SANTHANUTHALAPADU
nnrwh1975@gmail.com
9490742134

My Heart Beat

Madhav

Nuthalapati Nageswara Rao's writing career is long. He had the experience of writing down his feelings from his student days, reaching out to the readers and listeners through various magazines, media gaining their admiration.

The sense of progress that had sprouted from childhood expanded with him and he grew up to the point of questioning the superstitions rooted in the society till then. Nageswara Rao has written many works that direct the attention of the society towards change.

This volume is a collection of stories published in the same order.

"Kathala Kadambam" was published in Telugu language and created immense readership. It is a well-intentioned attempt to reach a global readership "The Beating Heart"

Anglicism. Fifteen of these stories are unique. It is remarkable that there is no closeness or similarity between any two stories.

If the stories were written about budding love between a young man and a young man, or including family scenes, we would not have to say anything special about these.

Each character tries to tell the reader something good. Every story aspires to a social purpose, indicates a solution. Their writing style goes on to make the readers understand that the practice without knowing the meaning becomes evil, even though atheism and rationalism sound the same. There is a vast difference between two. One revolves around the fact that there is no God. Another is to study everything in depth and ask why? What? How? It raises questions. The author's thoughts are filled with rationalism. It provokes thoughts in the readers.

As for the stories, even if they run along the letters with a fun style on the surface, there is a sensitive observation and research towards the society.

Coming to some of the stories:

THE SKY IS HIGH:
The quality of patience of the wife who never retorts to the husband who insults her with words every now and then without valuing the wife's love and services is visible. Finally, he ruthlessly left her, who did not know the value of a wife. It is interesting to see what decision the wife, who had lost her patience, took.

LOTUS FEET OF HUSBAND:
It has been newly discovered what kind of consequences the thoughts that are vaguely raging in the innermost part of a woman become reality. One wonders if she would be so angry with her husband even if she bears it in silence.

RIDGE GOURD BIRYANI:
A special story to be mentioned. No matter how grown up children may seem, they are always small in front of their parents. Unless they know the superiority of parents themselves, they never say it in front of their children. Confused that his generation was ahead of the curve in technology, he ended up being awestruck when he introduced it to his mother. Patiently heard everything the son had to say, but the mother did not try to tell her story. Until the son finds out on his own. Although the story is short and funny, it reflects the mind-sets and ways of thinking of parents and children.

JATKA:
It is clear that the author has given more importance to the things he wants to say through the characters in the story than the scenes between them. The halal of Muslim rituals which are generally not touched by anyone is explained in a way that everyone can understand. Also mentions the proximity between

the Jatka ritual of Hindus - Halal Key. This is really the answer to many people's doubts.

DOLLY THE PET:
The plot is serious. There is nothing wrong with loving animals and pets. Could it take priority over the care of the children? Can those born at a young age be rejected? The author has left it to the imagination of the readers.

This is a story where the reader should be self-critical.

BOND OF LOVE:
There are no more scenes in the story, no more unexpected twists. However, the two or three scenes that exist have wonderfully revealed human relationships, especially the love between mother and child. What did the unconscious mother say when she called her son to come to her in bed? What did you want from your son? What do parents want from their children in the end? Warm love, soulful touch. He heartily explained how upset they would be if they did not get the same. No matter how old you are, the reader is impressed by the way the author says that they should set aside a few moments in their busy schedule to greet their loved ones.

CADAVER TUB:
It is a distinct social phenomenon. The whole story seems like a story between father and son, but the father's thought, the ultimate meaning of insisting his son to take up the medical profession, his physical absence makes the reader's eyes melt at once. It is natural that when the soul merges into the infinite gases, the body wants to merge into the Five demons. You have to read and know what that father thought differently.

MANGO FRUITS:
A fun natural story. The author brazenly says that even if we do many wrongly chosen and unrecognized things in our lives, our inner soul keeps warning us.

Having said that, all the rest of the stories are anecdotal. Read again and again. Dinner is ahead. How much longer? Read on. Enjoy it.

My views as an illustrator who has read the 15 stories thoroughly and made a picture for them. I am grateful to Nuthalapati Nageswara Rao who gave me the opportunity to share my feelings with the readers.

My best wishes to him and wishing that many more such wonderful works of social utility come out from his bottom of the heart through his pen and usher in the change of society.

16 August, 2023
Hyderabad

Yours
Madhav
+91 7799882163

Table of Contents

BOND OF LOVE

Raghava was very happy to get a new job and he put in all his certificates in his bag.

He told his mother "Mom, I will have to start now. Bless me" saying this, he touched her feet reverentially.

"Be alert and fare well in your fresh job. Your father would have been immensely happy had he been here now with us" his mother blessed him.

Raghava was moved by taking blessings from his mother and get emotional eyes were filled with tears.

Raghava could not get the love and affection of his father as he passed away when Raghava was barely two years old. Raghava's mother had to do several odd jobs including house maid cooking, tailoring etc., and faced severe hardships, encouraging Raghava for good education and comfortable living.

Whenever Raghava was recollecting all those moments of hardships and difficult times, tears started rolling down his cheeks.

"Dear child ! Do a good job and get good name and fame in your office" blessed his mother.

"Sure Mom" said Raghava and stepped out. But his mother came out of their house and walked towards Raghava as an auspicious omen.

Raghava controlled his emotions with difficulty and walked towards the Bus Stand.

Raghava suddenly woke up from his deep thoughts and memories with the call of his wife Lalitha with a cup of coffee in her hands.

He started sipping the coffee but was unable to come out of the memories of his first day in the office.

Though he did not relish the old memories of his work in the job during subsequent days, months and years, whenever he recollected the incidents of hard times, they faced the good care his mother took in ensuring the comfortable life, without allowing any scope of discomfort and dissatisfaction. She brought him up with her inspiring and consoling words till he settled in a good job for his livelihood. He became emotional.

Those memories had been haunting him.

His wife Lalitha was too good in her nature and took good care of Raghava and the children. Somehow, he felt that she did not pay sufficient attention towards his mother. He also guilt that he was not taking proper care of his mother.

With the increase of her age, his mother's health was deteriorating. He got done a surgery to her heart when advised by the doctors. She had been a diabetic and he had been getting good treatment for it from a competent doctor.

Despite all these, Raghava felt, he was yet to do something for his mother and felt uncomfortable that he was not extending enough care and love towards his mother. When he shared his feelings with his wife, she consoled him saying that they were giving his mother timely food, medicines, clothing etc, and nothing else was needed to be given. Raghava though he had immeasurable and inexplicable love and affection towards his mother, he did not know how to express the same to her. When he expressed the same to his mother that he was not taking required care of her and asked to forgive him, she smiled and preferred to be calm without any reply to him. Such her silence made Raghava further pensive. She never asked him to show her to a doctor even when she was unwell. She had always been engaging herself with some household work or the other.

He recollected that his mother sacrificed her entire physical energy for his comfort and happiness.

But he felt that he was not reciprocating upto his level of satisfaction and felt further sad for this deed. He could not convince himself the reasons for this was not want of time or something else.

He was unable to convince himself why this was going on in an unsatisfactory manner. He decided at least from now he should talk to his mother with care and concern showering love and affection, and to spare some time for her daily.

He came to the senses with a call by his wife for dinner. He moved silently to the dining table and simultaneously looked towards his mother who was lying on the cot looking very dull, feeble without any movements. He got up from the dining table and walked towards his mother wishing to talk to her and get her affectionate caressing. His wife reminded him "You can always talk to your mother, but please have dinner first". Ignoring her word, Raghava moved a few steps towards his mother when she signaled him to sit on her cot. It was long time since he was sitting by his mother so affectionately. His eyes became wet and he enquired with her, "Mom, how are you? Did you take the porridge, your medicines and how do you feel now? Are you comfortable?" Mother placed her hands with Raghava hands and silently, gracefully looking into the already wet eyes of Raghava.

It was a pure unsullied flow of love to him. The feeling of love was as vast as a deep sea and gave a beautiful experience to his otherwise heavy heart. She remained silent and was not uttering anything. But the mom's love and concern did not allow him to move from there. The feeling of lovely bond could not be described or explained as it can only be felt and experienced. He started realizing how much he missed his mother till then. Mother was showering love and its mesmerism on him. He, for a moment, forgot everything with the flow of eternal indescribable pure love around him. Her fragile hands dropped down from the grip of his hands.

He screamed with pain from the bottom of his heart and through the inner spaces of his mind. The love of a mother can never be explained by the words that the lips can speak and utter. The vocabulary of a man failed in describing it.

The bond of love surrounded Raghava and she left to her heavenly abode. But the pure love of his mother inspires the scintillating feelings her dear son Raghava who started crying bitterly holding her in his hands and placing his head on her divine feet.

*

MANGO FRUITS

"*Kousalyaa Suprajaa Raama Poorvaa Sandhyaa Pravartate!*"

Kutumba Rao was enjoying the ceremonial wake up chanting of Lord Venkateswara without getting up from the bed.

His wife Saraswathi was on her loud voice awakened Kutumba Rao from his sleep.

"Please do not disturb me, Let me enjoy my sleep, peacefully for some time more" said Kutumba Rao still drowsy with his inadequate sleep.

"Enough is enough. Be happy that because of my prayers and rituals you remain healthy and bereft of diabetese, hyper tensions and so on. You have so many responsibilities to be accomplished like building our own house, performing the marriage of our dear daughter etc. It is not the time to prolong your sleep now. Please get ready and go for your morning walk,"

said his wife. "Yes, Do not worry. I am fine" murmuring slowly, Kutumba Rao got up from the bed and walked towards the rest room.

He made it a point to enjoy his wife's frequent reminders and sweet scoldings as the pleasant hymns of Bhagavadgeeta and the celestial wake up chantings. He firmly believed that he could not win the arguments with his dear wife and it was better to keep silence and compromise with her for a smooth run of family life.

Saraswathi sincerely loved her husband but got irritated for his, not offering any assistance in the daily chores. Even when he came forward to help her, the perfection misses and he did not pay enough attention to the task.

The Other day when she requested him to make *dosas,* he messed up the whole thing by using *roti* pan for dosas resulting in extra work of cleaning the pans. Naturally, she shouted at him for his ignorance about the difference between the *roti* and *dosa* pans.

In fact, Saraswathi proved always right in her decisions and deeds and that was the reason he prefered to keep silence for his errors and mistakes in the home front. He did not venture to oppose or criticize Saraswathi, since he was fully aware that she does everything in the correct manner even without involving himself.

"You are so unsuccessful in homely affairs and how you are going to be successful in the office" shouts Saraswathi. Kutumba Rao simply smiles it away. Maybe he made it a habit to laugh it off instead of feeling unpleasant.

Saraswathi reminded him to get ready and to go for the morning walk. Her words were so soothing to him, he took a bath and started for the morning walk.

She was surprised, "Why did you take a shower now before your morning walk as you should have it after returning from the walk?"

He realised his mistake and moved out of his house towards the park in the colony.

Sankara Rao was a friend of him and they both started walking together chatting and exchanging their opinions "You are lucky Kutumba Rao for your wife, who does systematic, spiritual and devotional prayers which resulted in getting a government job to your daughter" said Sankara Rao.

Kutumba Rao felt irked that all good things happened were due to Saraswathi only and he had no role in the eyes of others. He felt unhappy for the outsiders to think in the same lines as his family members did.

"Is it so, Sankara Rao? That means your wife is not doing the sufficient prayers because of which your son did not get admission in the university?" retorted Kutumba Rao.

"It differs from person to person. What my wife could do when my son did not get good marks and good rank in his examinations?" Sankara Rao tried to convince with his logic.

"Say so, Sankara Rao! Let us not argue on these issues. Let us walk further to maintain our good health" warned

Kutumba Rao.

He never opposes his wife in doing her prayers and performing devotional procedures at home. But it was true and he concurs that she takes the right and suitable decisions in family matters and about his maintaining good physical health. She had taken good care and paid necessary attention in all respects. If the family was happy and the life goes on smoothly, the entire credit must go to his wife Saraswathi only. He felt proud of his wife's competency.

In fact, Kutumba Rao was an atheist. He never believed in good virtues, bad omens even from his childhood but never dared to oppose or argue with his wife on those issues. Though he agreed with them, it was his weakness and he sometimes felt happy and contented.

Even while walking, several thoughts were engulfing him. Somehow, he completed his morning walk and returned home.

"Please get ready quickly and enjoy the delicious *Puries* that I made especially for your breakfast" said his wife Saraswathi.

Though Kutumba Rao could not distinguish the underlyning tone of his wife calling him for the breakfast as soft and affectionate or hard and criticism filled, but for sure it was certainly soothing kind and consoling for him.

He would be saying that he entered the washroom while she made some *Puris* with Potato curry and kept it ready on the dining table.

He came to the dining table, took a seat and started having the delicious Puries for his break fast.

She observed and pointed, "You had neither invited me to share the breakfast along with you nor at least appreciated my preparation of the puries" He simply smiled at her affectionately.

"Dear husband! It is now the season for mangoes specially of sweet *Banginapalli* mangoes. Please get some of them home before   the season is over"

"Sure, dear Saraswathi, I will certainly get them to you as soon as possible from the market" assured Kutumba Rao.

"At least after partaking the *puries* you could have let me have a word of appreciation how the preparation was. You never had such a habit" she chided.

"Yes the *puries* are really delicious and I enjoyed them" Having said so, he took a jute bag and started towards the market.

He enquired with a fruit dealer about the price of a dozen mangoes. The shopkeeper immediately retorted "Are you new to this market? We sell mangoes in kilos and not in dozens like in the olden days"

Kutumba Rao got irritated as to what it was this, even here outside his home too, he was not getting enough value and respect.

"That is all right. Please give me 3 kgs of good quality mangoes" told Kutumba Rao.

After buying the mangoes he straightly returned home and handed over the mangoes to his wife.

She was surprised and explained "You came very fast and by the grace of God you brought very good mangoes too" she commended.

Kutumba Rao was immersed in his own world of thoughts and started loitering in his room. After a little while he took a book from the bookshelf and laid down on his bed. A little later after reading a few pages of the book, he slipped into a short nap.

"Where are you ? I told you to get the provisions from the shop and I already made a list of those items," shouted his wife.

He got out of bed and took the list and jute bag with a grudge for not allowing him to rest peacefully.

While walking through the colony, he noticed that several mango trees are full of mangoes. Though he saw them daily, the fact of his buying them from the market pinched his heart.

He saw some old slippers hung to the mango trees near the fruits. The fruits were easily reachable to pluck and were very luring and tempting. What happens if I pluck them? The weather is little hot and no one is in the vicinity. How anyone could know if I pluck some of the luring mangoes?" As soon as he got this thought he laid his hands on the mangoes to pluck them from the branches.

He plucked a few mangoes and put them in his bag. He heaved a sigh of relief since nobody saw him plucking the fruits and nobody was seen in and around.

He went to the grocery store, bought groceries, put them in another bag and started back towards his home.

He was thinking what he should say to his wife about these new mangoes plucked from the tree and lying inside the bag.

He convinced himself, it is O.K. I can say anything to her. He kept the bag of mangoes below his cot in the bed room.

"I brought all the items as per your list and you can arrange them in the kitchen shelves " he told.

"Did you bring everything correctly? Did you bring Bansi ravva or Bombay ravva?" she asked him. "I brought *Bombay ravva*" he replied.

"What is this? you never pay any attention to what I need and what I wrote in the list. What is the use? You do not know even how to get the groceries properly" chided his wife.

He, as usual, smiled at her and assured her "O.K. I will get it replaced" having said, he went back to the shop replaced the ravva and returned home.,

At home he rested for a while with the television and the day came to dusk. His wife asked him whether he prefers to have rice or chapati for his dinner.

"As you wish" said Kutumba Rao. He finished his dinner and started thinking about the mangoes in the bag. He laid on his bed and closed his eyes. After completing the dometic chores, Saraswathi too joined him on the bed and pointed

"How come you are so tired and exhausted? "

As usual he took it light and smiled.

He felt very discomfortable and couldn't get sleep. He was simply tossing on his bed for a long time. Somehow with great difficulty he fell asleep very late in the night. While in the deep sleep, he saw a night mare in which he saw a black cobra hanging from the branches of the mango tree from which he plucked the few mangoes holding the old torn slipper in its mouth. It was slapping him with the old and torn slipper on his cheeks number of times.

"Snake, slipper, slipper in its mouth, the devil, slapping my cheeks! Oh my God, it is slapping on my cheeks" he started shouting, while closing eyes with fear on his face.

Saraswathi got up from the bed and looked at her husband. He got up suddenly and started shivering with fear. He pulled his bed sheet to his waist and sat on the bed with continuous shivering.

Then it struck to his mind why the owners of the mango trees in the colony hang the old and torn slippers and shoes to the trees with fruits.

Saraswathi shook his shoulders with both her hands and enquired,"What happened? why are you so petrified? why are you trembling-? Have some water and be calm. Do not worry. Everything will be fine." she assured and gave him a glass of water and made him to drink it.

If Saraswathi came to know about the mangoes below the cot, what will happen? With this thought he started shivering further.

"She may not like and she may not tolerate. She may shout at me and curse me"

The fear engulfed him like a devil and it made him further fearful and the shivering aggravated.

*

MATCH MAKING

"**D**on't worry! Be happy, Get ready fast. This time the match will be final. You need not feel that what happened earlier will repeat. The seekers' family is distantly related to us. The Groom to be has a good job with a hefty income. He is tall and handsome, humble and obedient to his parents. Even the horoscopes of you both matched as well. So, you do not think adversely unnecessarily!" Govindamma encouraged her elder daughter Lakshmi but Lakshmi remained unmoved.

She simply smiled a bit at her mother but thought herself "I should not be greedy and overambitious. Who will come forward to marry this dark girl?"

She sat silently before the dressing table. Her younger sister Saraswathi came and told her mother that the family of the groom reached the town, they will offer their prayers in the local temple and later they would visit their home. It was not going to be late.

She assured her sister, "Lakshmi! Don't worry, this time your match will certainly get fixed"

Lakshmi felt unhappy as she knew that her younger sister was fair in her complexion and was good-looking. Any boy who looks at her would immediately like her and admire her. It was not her fault to be born dark but she has to face the unpleasant events.

This was the fourth time match coming but the result was unsuccessful.

Her mother reminded Lakshmi again to get ready fast to meet the guests for match making.

"Yes Mom! I am always positive and take everything easy. Somehow, you want to get me married and send me out of the home. If my marriage is performed, then the younger one will get a good match very easily and comfortably. Then Mom will be satisfied having completely fulfilled her family responsibilities"

Saraswathi came forward to get Lakshmi ready with an attractive attire and a suitable make up. Lakshmi resisted saying that she does not want any extra efforts to present herself look impressive. She said cynically "I do not want to apply even the normal face powder now. You are beautiful and any one can easily marry you!"

"O.K. My dear sister! I will marry only after you get married. But now you have to get ready as the guests are expected to be here now or any moment" Saraswaathi tried to convince her.

Mother Govindamma consoled Lakshmi, "If the groom looks at you in the auspicious time, he will certainly like you. You keep smiling and be comfortable with yourself. We will look after the other activities"

Saraswathi too added, "I am confident this alliance will surely be finalized" with her affectionate looks at her elder sister.

"Say so! Then you wish to enjoy your turn once my marriage is over!" chided Lakshmi.

Meanwhile, the Pundit came there and advised that it was the auspicious time and Lakshmi can join the guests. He suggested the bridegroom to look at the bride.

Groom's mother looked at Lakashmi and desired to put her into conversation. But Lakshmi mistook that it was the beginning of the future domination of the would be mother-in-law. Anyway, why to presume all these? Slowly, Lakshmi lifted her eye lids and looked at the groom Suresh. He looked good but can such a good-looking and handsome man can approve me? were her inner thoughts.

She further observed that Suresh's looks were not on her, guessed who got his attention. She immediately thought, "Oh, even this trial goes off. I may have to get ready for the 5th time subsequently"

The pundit interfered and initiated some conversation with both the families. Suresh preferred to remain silent as his attention was somewhere else.

His mother too initiated a chit chat with Lakshmi but for a short while.

Lakshmi slowly got up from her seat and served sweets and condiments to the guests. She felt continuously pessimistic that she may not be the suitable bride to this handsome Suresh.

The guests got up and told that they would convey their opinion after going back to their home and after discussing among themselves. They took leave off from the father of Lakshmi.

Lakhmi suspected that it was a clue for her non acceptability and moved slowly to her bed room with tears rolling down her cheeks.

Govindamma tried to console Lakshmi that the horoscopes matched well indicating that the marriage would be finalised and that it was the opinion of the Pundit too.

Saraswathi too tried to encourage Lakshmi about the possibility of this match getting finalised.

After a few days, Pundit came home and mentioned that Suresh liked Saraswathi to marry but preferred to wait till Lakshmi's marriage took place.

He wondered how his predictions could go wrong as the horoscopes made a good match.

"I knew it very well. It is my fate. Why do you blame the horoscopes?" Lakshmi retorted thinking sorrowfully.

Veerabhadram, father of Lakshmi also expressed his unhappiness that the fate of Lakshmi was not favorable resulting in such developments.

Later Saraswathi secured a job.

"Let Saraswathi do the job for some time. Unless the elder one gets married the younger one can't follow the line. This is the fourth time that the match does not get finalised for poor Lakshmi as her fate appears to be unlucky. " Veerabhadram wiped his tears. On an auspicious time, Govindamma prompted her younger daughter Saraswathi to report for the new job. Saraswathi got ready, touched her parents' feet reverentially and took leave of her sister Lakshmi. She reached her office reported to her higher authorities and sent a message in WhatsApp, to her parents and her sister and then opened her lap top starting her office work.

During the lunch time, she took her lunch box to the canteen which was in the second floor of the building. There she noticed Suresh who came to their home to approve Lakshmi. Why was he here? What was he doing here? He should be blasted for what he did to her family.

Suresh too saw Saraswathi, got surprised and wished her, 'Good Morning.' Saraswathi was furious. Why did he do that way? Having come to see Lakshmi how could he like me? She could not control her anguish over Suresh and asked him.

"What is this? Why are you following me?"

Suresh replied "My office is in this floor. Having seen you in your home I liked you very much in the first instance itself. Now we both are working in the same office. If we marry each other, it will be convenient to both of us. Even I can convince my parents for our marriage"

"I am, no doubt, fair in my complexion but I am not good at cooking. My sister is an expert in cooking apart from being good at classical music. She may be dark in colour but does it prohibit my sister from getting married to you "Saraswathi questioned Suresh. "In fact we already informed that she is dark to your family. Knowing it fully well rejecting her and liking me is totally unfair on your part!"

Suresh could not answer. The introspection began in his mind resulting in disturbed attention to his office work.

"Being an educated and cultured person, how could I prefer the beauty and attraction of the body? My father was fair but my mother was not so fair in her complexion. When the discrimination did not crop up between my parents about the colour how could I think in such a discriminating manner? When my mother saw Lakshmi indeed, she had a word of appreciation to her. How could I not think in the way my mother saw the situation"

He started realizing his foolish behavior and became pensive in his moods. He reached his home later.

At home, when he initiated discussion his father Subbarayudu expressed his unpleasantness over the way the things happened. This made Suresh lost in thoughts.   Even after good education, nice manners and rational thinking, how could anyone discriminate about the mere color of the body and not the heart inside? Was it not unwarranted and unethical? Going to see a girl but approving a different girl and proposing to her? His conscience did not permit to compromise on the human values. Saraswati was right in her words. He started feeling guilty in his heart of hearts.

Next morning, when Lakshmi looked at her mobile WhatsApp messages a message from Suresh attracted her attention.

"I am sorry. Please pardon me. My parents will be reaching your home shortly to decide and fix the auspicious date for our marriage"

A happy and beautiful smile shined on her lips. She looked at Saraswathi who too reciprocated with a bigger smile in appreciation!

*

THE KEY

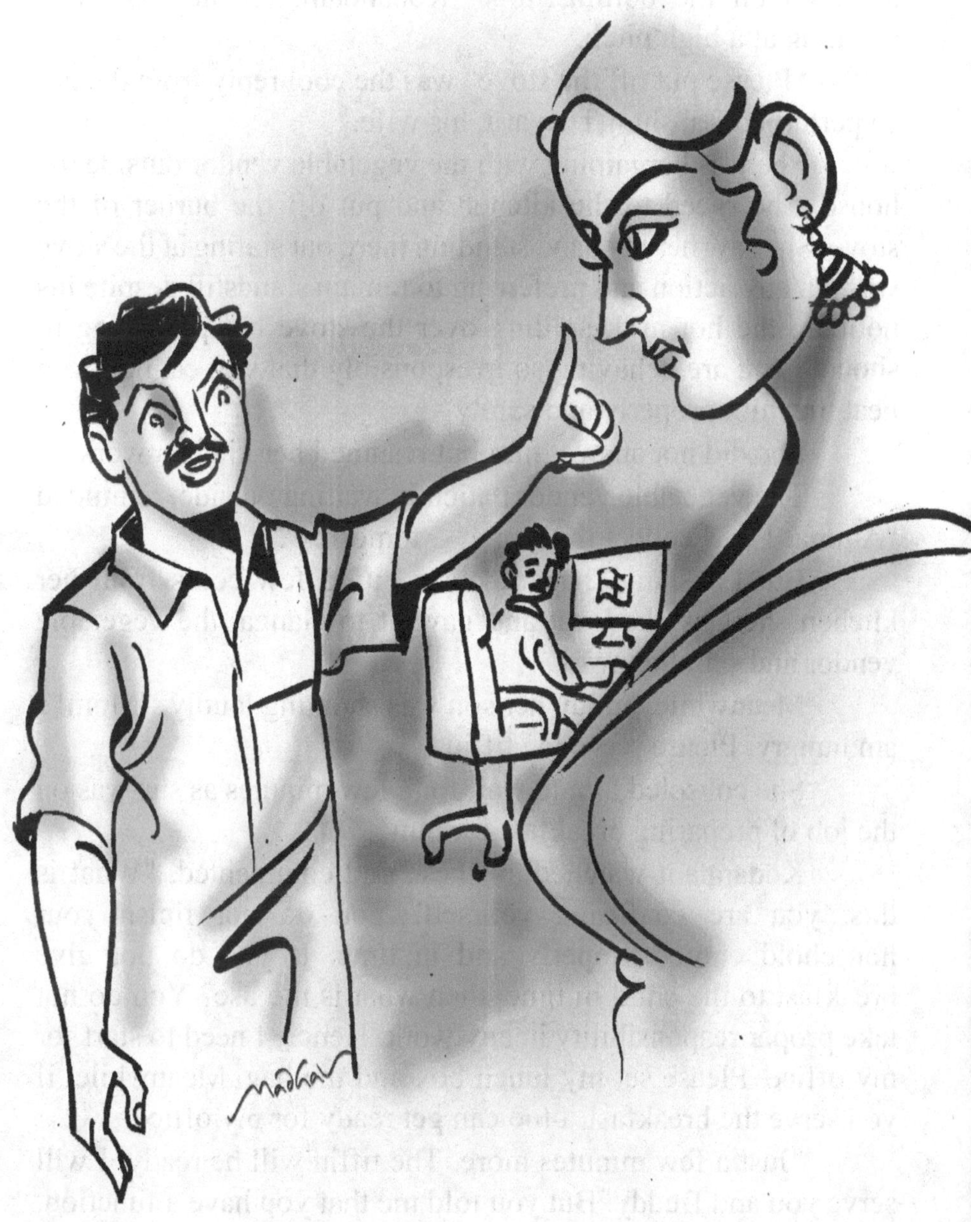

"Where are you Thayaru? Don't you look at the milk boiling and spilling on the stove? Don't you pay the slightest attention on the boiling milk" Kodandam, the husband was shouting at a high pitch.

"Please put off the stove" was the cool reply from the not so perturbed Lakshmi Thayaru, his wife.

She was bargaining with the vegetable vendor outside the house. She raced to the kitchen and put off the burner of the stove. She saw her husband standing there but staring at the stove without any action and preferring to remain standstill despite his noticing the hot milk spilling over the stove but preferring to shout, "You are behaving so irresponsibly that you cannot even heat the milk properly and safely"

She did not answer him but resumed her kitchen work.

The vegetable vendor patiently waiting outside, reminded "Amma! I will collect the money   tomorrow!"

But Lakshmi Thayaru picked up a few coins from her kitchen shelf, walked out and gave it to Ganga, the vegetable vendor and sent her away.

Meanwhile, buddy her son was shouting loudly, "Mom! I am hungry. Please serve me tiffin."

She consoled him to wait for a few minutes as she was on the job of preparing breakfast for him.

Kodandam watched all these and commented, "What is this, you are confusing yourself. You do not finish your household chores properly and in time. If you do not give breakfast to the child in time, then what is the use? You do not take proper responsibility in any work. Hence, I need to start for my office. Please set my lunch box and the bag. Meanwhile, if you serve the breakfast, I too can get ready for my office"

"Just a few minutes more. The tiffin will be ready. I will serve you and Buddy. But you told me that you have a function, at your office today and hence you need not carry your lunch box to the office" Thayaru reminded.

"That is again a clear irresponsibility on your part. I might have told you that I may not need the lunch box. You should have remained silent and did not prepare my lunch box. But you prefer to point it out unnecessarily. That is again an act of irresponsibility on your part" murmured Kodandam.

It has become a habit for him to criticize his wife frequently.

"Here is your breakfast and for Buddy too. Please have it" told his wife.

"Again, behaving so irresponsibly. You could have handed over the tiffin plate to me. I do not understand when you would learn how to respect your husband and when you will behave with proper responsibility?" Kodandam shouted and he continued his shouting at Buddy also, "How long you keep playing with the cell phone? Don't you feel responsible in your matters? Come and have your meal."

Buddy came out of his room, took his tiffin plate and returned to his bedroom.

While taking his tiffin Kodandam impatiently asked his wife, "What is this? You are not getting ready for the office. Is it not getting late for you too?" So irresponsible? Did you apply for leave for today?"

She got used to such irritating words from him, since her marriage. She had been silently bearing with such unpleasant words from him. She never tried to reply or counter his words. She has been patiently carrying on her family life.

"You start for your office. I need to have my bath and later, I will start for my office"

Even before she finished her words Kodandam retaliated" So irresponsible! You should have taken the bath and then started your household chores"

"Buddy! I am going for a bath and if my phone rings, please attend it" told the mother.

When she went inside the restroom, she heard her husband speaking loudly. She heard the sound of an auto rickshaw in front of her house.

She spoke loudly "Buddy! Please see. It seems someone came home. Please see that they are seated in the hall as daddy seems to be busy talking to someone else"

But Buddy did not pay attention to his mother's words as he was busy with his conference on line in his room.

After finishing her bath Lakshmi Thayaru came out saw no one there in the hall and felt relieved that no one came to visit then contrary to her presumption.

She got ready for the office and peeped through the door of the room to find her son Buddy. "Buddy today being Monday do not skip your lunch in your busy work. I kept it in the hot box keeping it warm. There are tasty curries and curd too. I won't be able to return home for lunch as there is audit going on in my office and hence me too is carrying my lunch box to my office"

"Yes Mom! I will" replied Buddy.

Lakshmi Thayaru reached her office and introduced herself to the team of auditors and assured her availability to the team.

"I will attend to your work and provide whatever the records you may require" she said and got herself busy in the office work.

She simultaneously advised the other office staff members to involve themselves fully and seriously in attending and the auditors and in showing the necessary records.

A Couple of hours passed and it was time for lunch. She called Somu the office attender to look after the lunch arrangements for the guests of audit party.

She opened her lunch box but suddenly remembered her lovely son Buddy and wondered whether he took his lunch or not. Her affection made her to take her mobile to call Buddy and to enquire.

Buddy replied in the affirmative and cautioned his mother about her health and to have lunch in time.

"Yes Buddy I am about to have it. I am busy with my audit work. It may be late for me to return home in the evening. When daddy comes home, please give some coffee to him and attend to him. He is short tempered and might be impatient. Please look after the home in all respects till I return home. On my arrival I will prepare the dinner"

"Sure Mom! I have the conference at 3'O' clock. I will attend to daddy and the home. You first have your lunch"

She got immersed in her thoughts about the sound of an auto rickshaw and her husband's voice in the morning. Who could it be that came by the auto? Or is it simply my fancy? Kodandam always murmurs and criticizes anything and everything.

On side, the stress of audit work and on the other, the irritating behavior of her husband went on disturbing her. Some how with all those conflicting thoughts she completed her lunch.

Kodandam too was not comfortable in his office. Lakshmi Thayaru was absolutely not taking any responsibility in the home affairs even after 24 years of his marriage. She did not feel like handing over the vehicle keys when he started towards the office from home.

"I had to take an auto rickshaw today for the office. She did not enquire over the phone how I reached my office"

He could not pay enough attention on his office work. How long this careless and irresponsible wife remains not learning the basics of running the family even after so many years of married life?

He attended the function in the lunch time but his mind was fully engaged with thoughts of making his wife understand the responsible way of running the family. He thought of scolding her over telephone but restrained himself that scolding her in person may prove to be more effective. At least then she will realize her mistakes and start correcting herself in a better and responsible way.

Lakshmi Thayaru finished her audit work and returned home by 6.30 in the evening. She looked for her husband in the house but in vain. She observed his motorbike parked in the compound. She could not reconcile that his bike was there but he was not to be seen in the house. It is certain that he was yet to reach home and heaved a sigh of relief that she could reach home earlier than her husband.

It rained heavily and Kodandam had to take an auto rickshaw from his office. He again recollected and murmured that his wife was so irresponsible in not handing over an umbrella to him despite that being rainy season.

He reached home fully drenched in the rain and came inside the house.

"Thayaru! How many times I need to remind you to feel responsible even to a slightest extent? Why could not you give me the vehicle keys when I started for my office? How could I blame you alone? It is my father to be blamed equally for getting you married to me. I had to go to my office in an auto rickshaw despite having a two-wheeler in the house!" Kodandam shouted at his wife.

Hearing the loud voice of his father, Buddy came out his room. Lakshmi Thayaru also came there from the kitchen. Both the mother and the son looked at Kodandam and his dress to be fully drenched and the resultant transparent pocket of his shirt with keys inside. Kodandam too observed them looking at his shirt pocket. Automatically his hands moved towards his pocket and got the touch of the keys there in his pocket!

His face turned pale! Thayaru and Buddy burst into laughter!

*

THE GARLIC

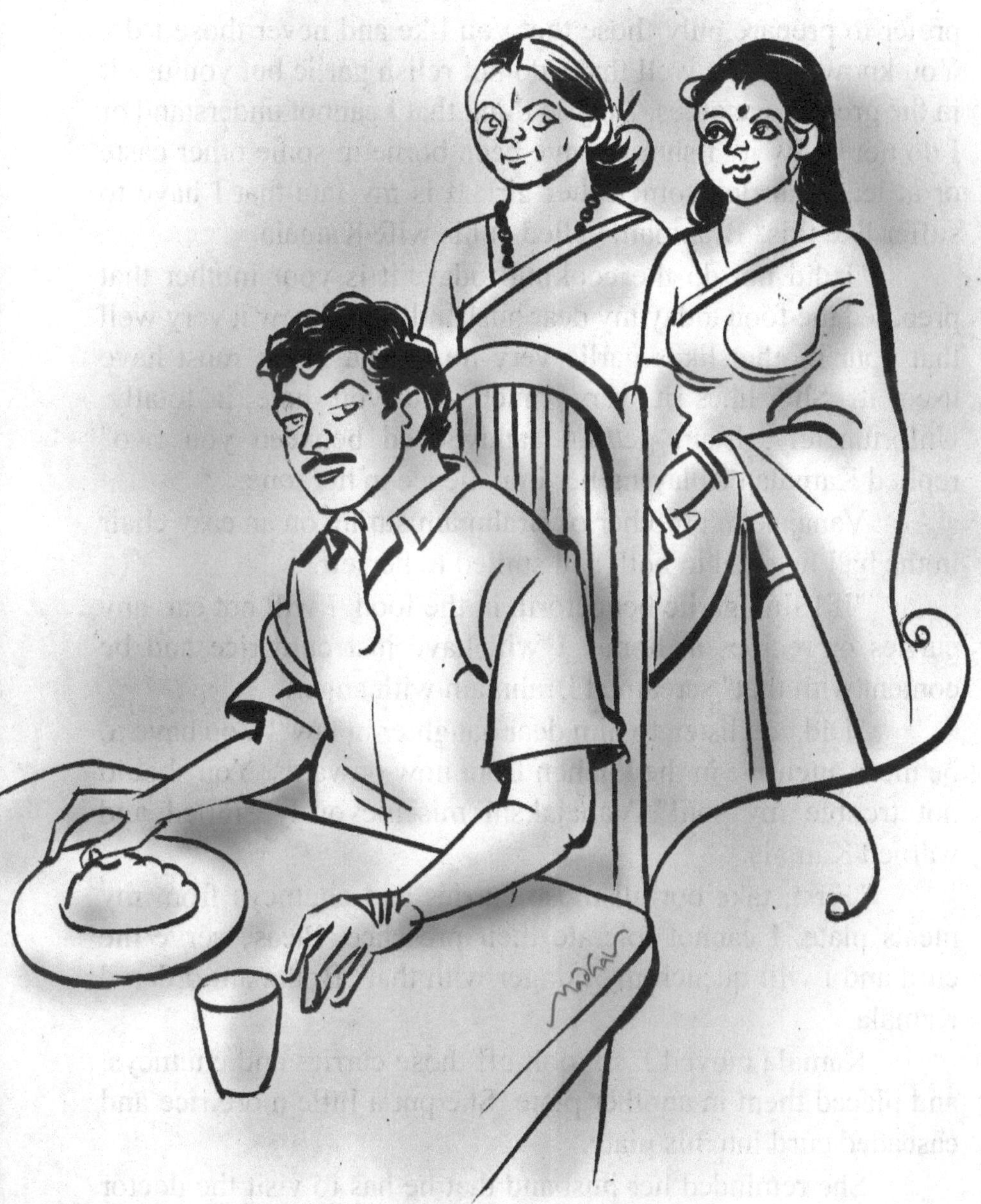

"How many times should I tell you? Even then you prefer to prepare only those that you like and never those I do. You know it pretty well that I do not relish garlic but you use it in the green vegetables. Do you think that I cannot understand or I do not know it? I should have been borne in some other caste or at least married some other girl. It is my fate that I have to suffer like this" Brahmam yelled at his wife Kamala.

"I did not do the cooking today. It is your mother that prepared the food today my dear husband! You knew it very well that your mother likes garlic very much and hence must have used it. She likes it very much and you hate it totally. Unfortunately, I am getting sandwiched between you two" replied Kamala displaying her impatience in her tone.

Vanajaksh, i mother of Brahmam sitting on an easy chair in the hall listened to both and smiled to herself.

"If I find garlic henceforth in the food, I will not eat any curries or recipes at home. I will have just curd rice and be content with that" screamed Brahmam with anger.

"Did you listen to him dear daughter in law ? You have to be more attentive in the kitchen from now onwards. You should not trouble my son!" Vanajakshi mischievously smiled and warned Kamala.

"First, take out all those curries and chutneys from my meals plate. I cannot tolerate their presence. Please serve me curd and I will quench my hunger with that" Brahmam ordered Kamala.

Kamala moved fast, took off those curries and chutneys, and placed them in another plate. She put a little more rice and cascaded curd into his plate.

She reminded her husband that he has to visit the doctor on empty stomach the next morning for a checkup and several other tests. She also added that he has to go to bed early for the next day visit to the doctor. She arranged his bed well and made him sleep early and consoled.

"It is O.K, I remember that. You and mother should have your food. Now Mother! You should be careful about your health" he said while moving to his bed room.

Vanajakshi told Kamala, "You have to be cautious while serving him food. He somehow detected the garlic in the food. I cannot convince him daily"

"It is O.K, Mother in law! From tomorrow onwards I will not use garlic in the food. I won't even mention it in the list of groceries to be brought" Kamala uttered a bit louder so that Brahmam too could hear it.

"What is this Kamala? I cannot relish anything without garlic. He dislikes it totally. At least in this fag end of my life let me have my likes and pleasures!" Vanajakshi softly reminded Kamala.

"Do not worry Mother in law! How can I do it so and displease you? Somehow, I will ensure that he doesn't find it next" Kamala affectionately assured Vanajakshi.

"You are so nice. But be careful. I know that I will not be deprived of garlic in your presence. But I also caution you that you should not trouble my son" Vanajakshi caressed Kamala.

"Yes, you both are so dear to me like mine own eyes" replied Kamala.

"That I know very well. Now serve me the food. You can put all that garlic even from your plate in mine. I like it so much that I am glad to have it more today" told Vanajakshi.

"Fine! Take them all" and Kamala served sumptuous garlic to her mother-in-law along with rice and other recipes. She gave some garlic from her portion of the food also to her mother-in-law to make her happy. Vanajakshi felt very happy with the tasty food with lots of garlic. She felt thankful for those who discovered garlic for such pleasant usage.

Next morning Brahmam got up very early, went to the laboratory, and gave the samples of his blood and urine for various tests. The lab technician advised Brahmam to go for breakfast and give the blood samples within an hour after having his breakfast.

Brahmam returned to his house observed that his mother was busy in the kitchen with food preparation and commented "Mother, why did you start cooking today? Where is Kamala and what is she doing?"

" Dear son! I decided to cook food today especially for you and hence I am myself in the kitchen," told Vanajakshi. She enquired about his visit to the doctor.

"I need to have my breakfast and go back to the lab for giving the samples for the post prandil results" replied Brahmam.

"Fine! I prepared delicious *dosas* for you. Please have them and then go for the tests" she advised him and then served *dosas* to him.

He comfortably consumed four of them and appreciated his mother for the tasty preparations and her cooking mastery in general.

Later, he went to the laboratory and waited for his turn for the tests for an hour before giving his blood samples. He patiently waited for the reports of the tests and then visited the doctor with the reports.

The clinic was fully crowded and Brahmam's turn came around at 1 O' clock in the afternoon. Doctor examined Brahmam, perused his reports checked his blood pressure and advised "You need to take the bliood pressure tablets, regularly and you need to control your cholesterl too. You need to have these tests once in a quarter. Further more, you make it a habit to take a walk at least for half an hour daily. Please consume some garlic every morning. You can use garlic in your food, *curries, chutneys* etc which will control your cholesterol and your blood pressure"

Brahmam could not digest the advice of the doctor on the usage of garlic. Maybe he thought the doctor did not know his repulsion towards garlic and convinced himself.

He came back home and threw the reports on the center of the table impatiently. Looking at his unpleasant behavior his mother enquired, "What happened and what are the findings of the doctor?" Kamala too enquired him about the doctor's advice.

Brahmam did not reply and sat silently in his chair. His mother understood his position. Kamala brought a glass of butter milk and offered him. He coolly took it and drank. He observed interesting flavors are emanating from the kitchen. So, it is the mother that is cooking today and hence it should be tasty with beautiful fragrances he thought for himself.

Kamala advised him to have a bath and get ready for lunch so that his mother would serve him food.

Brahmam got ready and came to the dining table waiting for the tasty preparations by his mother. They will always be very tasty and full of mouthwatering flavors and fragrances. It does not mean to underestimate the cooking of his wife Kamala. She too does it systematically and tastily.

"Do not worry my son, you have to maintain your good health. Blood pressure is not a disease" his mother said to him.

"It will be controlled" she added.

He was surprised at her words. How did she know about his high blood pressure? Might be it was the affection of the mother to understand the son in all respects he wondered in his heart of hearts.

Vanajakshi served hot food rice and some curries, sat with him and advised him to partake it.

He checked all the curries with his right index finger and felt relieved, as he did not get any garlic in them. The food was indeed very tasty and he enjoyed consuming it. He felt it was very tasty, tastier than ever before. He observed Kamala through the corners of his eye lids to note her feelings while his mother served a little more of the curries and other condiments to him.

Brahmam was extremely happy to have the delicious food. He quenched his hunger totally and went inside the bed room for a small nap.

Vanajakshi and Kamala too had their lunch looked and smiled at each other. After the nap Brahmam got out of his bed. He started feeling very light and comfortable as if he is floating in the air. He felt very happy.

He asked his wife Kamala to get the blood pressure checking machine. She brought it immediately and fixed the band to his left hand to check his blood pressure. Interestingly Brahmam found the readings very normal as those of a normal healthy person.

Vanajakshi looked at her son with smiling face. He is so innocent just like his father. He could not notice the garlic which was made a paste and mixed in the curries. Brahmam who otherwise disliked garlic, silently and unknowingly consumed enough garlic in the food resulting in bettering his health. She was very happy and amused with her son's attitude. Kamala, knowing the reason joined Vanajakshi in smiling.

Brahmam innocently but happily smiled at Kamala and Vanajakshi.

*

RIDGE GOURD BIRYANI

"Dear Raghava! How long do you spend your time with your damn mobile phone? You may be doing a software job but it does not mean that you should always be fully engaged with your laptop and mobile phone. At least when you are at home, please keep conversing with us" Mother, Savitri expressed her dissatisfaction over her son with a slightly louder voice.

"It is not so, Mom! Now, tell me how I can help you!" Raghava came out of his mobile phone and consoled his mother. He continued "Mom, I am going through E-Books, which is very convenient and almost free. Nowadays, all my friends and colleagues do go through E-Books only" , saying so,

he came out and looked for his mother but could not find her.

"Mom, where are you?"

"I'm in kitchen, dear"

Hearing the reply from his mother, Raghava proceeded to the kitchen and he offered to help her in cooking the lunch.

"You spend hardly two days at home and even these two days, can't you spare for your parents ? " Once you go back to your job, you automatically immerse in your own different world altogether. If you continue this way, even after your marriage, how is it going to be smooth? " Mother expressed her anguish.

Raghava, interrupted his mother's words and repeated his offer for help in cooking.

"How can you help me in cooking? Has your dad helped me all these years? Now you are ready to fill that gap" she uttered harshly. Raghava smiled at his mother's anger.

"Mom, You have been very busy all along in the kitchen and let me explain, how to do the cumbersome household work, very easily, with the help of my mobile. Now, coming to the point, what exactly do you want to do now "? Raghava convincingly asked his mother.

She laughed at his words and observed, "Whatever I prepare for you, eat it and enjoy it and that itself is a big help to me"

"That is nice of you, Mom, I will certainly take whatever you prepare so lovingly and tasteful Deliciously But I will definitely show you how anyone can easily follow the guidance from You Tube, to prepare things very easily." Raghava explained his mother.

"That is good to know. However, I prepared this spicy *Pongal*, please partake it along with your father. " She served the delicious *pongal*, in two plates and invited her husband too, to taste of it.

Sivaram, her husband, took his seat at the dining table and commented, "Savitri, you always prefer to prepare, everything, that Raghava likes and enjoys, as soon as he comes home, from Hyderabad. You always keep enquiring, what he likes for his breakfast, what he would have in the lunch, dinner, etc., and serve him those so affectionately thus giving importance to him and not me!"

"Please, do not say so, he is alone in Hyderabad, forced to take all and sundry, in his food, without proper tastes. Such food, spoils his appetite and health too. Once he gets married, his wife will look after his food needs and serve him tasty food. At least, when he is here, for the weekends, let him have, whatever he prefers and likes. It will be my pleasure to prepare all those items" Savitri explained, supporting Raghava.

Sivaram nodded in conformity and started taking the *Pongal*. Raghava too appreciated his mother about the tasty dish. " Mother does everything very tasty. There in the mess, in Hyderabad, the food is routine, bland, boring and never delicious. I cannot enjoy there thoroughly and that is the reason, I come home, once in a week to enjoy Mom's cooking"

"You always praise your mother, that too, even before you try the dish. "Sivaram laughed at Raghava.

Savitri looked sheepishly at her husband and said, " Did you ever help me in the kitchen? See now, our son, though very busy reading his books, is coming forward to help his mother."

" Is it so, ? If he starts helping you, in cooking, I should lose all my hopes on my food today" Sivaram threw a suspicious look at his wife and son.

After Sivaram finished his breakfast, Savitri went into the kitchen, kept aside, some portion of the spicy *Pongal* for the maid and ate the rest herself. She finished it and put all the vessels to be washed, in a plastic tray near the wash area. She saw her son, busy with his mobile and her husband appears to have gone out, as usual, without informing her.

She lost herself in her own thoughts and came out of them with the voice of her son. He offered to start cooking for lunch. She asked the maid, to relish the *Pongal* kept for her and then to complete washing of utensils. The maid finished her work and commended Savitri about the tasty *Pongal* she gave her.

Raghava took his mobile and initiated his mother to be ready. He offered to make a new dish and assured her, that he will participate in the cooking as well. He opened You Tube application in his mobile and got ready to prepare *Biryani* with Ridge gouard, a green vegetable. He showed all those materials required for preparation to his mother and started the process. Two ridge gouards, a few onion pieces, green chilies, garlic, spicy powders, *Basmati* rice etc., were all kept ready.

Raghava felt very happy that his mother was able to follow the instructions, with the help of the video in the You Tube.

"This saves a lot of time and I should train mother with at least two recipes every week." he thought.

She placed the rice in the pressure cooker and switched on the cooker. "You need to wait for two whistles, to come, " said Raghava.

The lady in the You Tube explains, what all are required, very clearly. But Savitri is doing all that was needed, very silently and systematically. This made him very happy. Even the cooking was about to come to a close.

Mother casually asked Raghava, "Which other recipes are present in your Mobile?"

"There are many more, Mom, I will explain one each, daily, to you" Raghava answered, feeling happy that he could assist his mother.

*****

The narration in the youtube came to close and the host thanked the viewers for watching the video. Raghava was astonished to see her in the Mobile as she was none other than Savitri, his own mother. He stared at her as he realized anew the value of her great art of cooking and its superior taste.

Raghava, so far, knew only to enjoy the delicacies made by his mother. He wondered, how, she, not only knows how to cook well, but to present, to share, what she does, on the You Tube.

Raghava, with his brightened eyes, wholeheartedly appreciated Savitri, his mother and she affectionately caressed him.

*

JATKA

Abdullah was very sad and started crying profusely, with no one to console him from his sadness. His uncle Karim tried, "Please control yourself, Abdullah! If you, such a learned and brave man, lose your heart so much, who can console your deeply broken mother and younger sister? Now it is your turn, to sustain and support your family. Be assured that we are always there with you. We may be a little away physically but my contact number was given to your mother, and so, I will always be available to you in case of need with just one phone call."

All the relatives, who came to share the irreparable loss, started slowly departing from the place, leaving Abdullah, a bit gloomy, confused, disturbed, and pensive.

Since his childhood Abdullah had been spending much time in Madarsa and was not much aware as to how his father was running their family and the several intrinsic difficulties and inconveniences in that process.

Since his father suddenly left for his heavenly abode, the responsibility of running the family naturally fell upon Abdullah now. It is very hard, to think about those things now and he was unable to control himself, as the mere thoughts were very disturbing.

"For a person like you, studying Quran, planning to become a religious preacher, enlightening several others for a disciplined and righteous life, to support your family and take up the requisite responsibilities, it cannot be difficult to control yourself and so please do not worry" said Suresh his childhood friend trying to console Abdullah. Those consoling words of Suresh appeared more comfortable than those of his relatives.

Though Abdullah is very young, he commands good respect in the local Muslim community. He mingles and moves with one and all.

He is a vegetarian and it is rare that a Muslim boy was preferring to be a vegetarian. His sincerity, humble behavior, simplicity, and good nature impress upon all the local people.

He does not involve in arguments and controversies. His whole world was *Madarsa* only and nothing else.

Since it was time for Namaz, Abdullah, went to the Masjid, finished his prayers, and returned home.

He checked with his mother, " Mother, could I go to *Madarsa* from tomorrow "?

"Please do so, Abdullah, whatever you feel to do, you can carry. It is all Allah's grace!" mother caressed Abdullah.

"Till now father ran the mutton shop, taking care of the family. Since he was not there now, I need to safeguard the family, take necessary care of the mother and support the education of the younger sister, and to perform her marriage with a suitable boy. I am not very much acquainted with elders in the village. I need to decide to take up some money earning activity"

Abdullah began to lose himself in several thoughts but was unable to come to any conclusion. He can decide to run the mutton shop like his father which might not be avoided. Engulfed with several thoughts which were never-ending, Abdullah completed his Namaz and returned to his home.

"Mother, I may run the mutton shop from tomorrow. I do not get any alternative idea for running the family. I will follow and continue the business like my father. Please bless me for success in my endeavor" Abdullah mentioned.

He set right the palm leaves façade for the shop? He cleaned the big wood log and sharpened the big knife. He swept up the flooring, sprinkled water, and cleaned it.

He went to his friend Suresh, and explained that he wished to continue the mutton shop. Like his father and he took his mother's consent too. Suresh laughed. "You never touch mutton, nor eat it. Have a second thought about your decision of running the mutton shop"

"Yes Suresh, I thought over it. I decided to continue the same work, as that of my father, for supporting my family. I do not find any alternative to support my family and to bridge the gap created by the absence of my father. You know everything about my hfamily," said Abdullah.

"It is O.K. I will certainly assist you in your shop till you settle down in your business and acquaint yourself with the business intricacies", Suresh assured Abdullah.

Abdullah felt very happy with the assurance from his friend to help him in establishing the business.

Suresh established his mutton shop and told Abdullah "Rasul who makes *Halal*, did not turn up till now. There may not be any sales today and so let us go home". Both started towards Abdullah's home. They found Rasul waiting at the mutton shop of Abdullah.

Rasul explained that he came to know that Abdullah is reopening the mutton shop and hence he came there.

"Before starting the sales, we have to do the halal to the chicken. Rasul does that job" Suresh continued.

Abdullah interrupted Suresh "Why *Halal* is to be done?"

"If we do *Halal*, before cutting the animal, no sin smites us and we have been following it since the times of my grandfather" Suresh explained.

"What is this ? No sin? How come? Even if we kill the live animal, no sin to us, just because, we performed *Halal*? The question arose in the heart of Abdullah.

Suresh continued, "Your father used to sell around 7 or 8 chicks daily. On Sundays, meat of other animals like, sheep, lamb etc., was sold. For making halal, of an animal, Rasul gets twenty-five rupees and for the chicken, he will get ten rupees each. I will send the worker from my shop, to you, for dressing the chicken, after halal, to fry it in the fire and other such needy works. There will be different rates for the skinless and with skin. The rates of birds fluctuate, every day. You need not go out for buying the chicken, as the supplier delivers the birds, at your door step. It is enough, if you give some advance money to the supplier and you can pay the balance amount, next day. You should never sell meat on credit, to the people. The waste materials like, the skin, bones etc., are all taken by some people, for making oil and other by products etc., from them. You must keep your shop always very clean and neat. Our village is a very small one and ours are the only two mutton shops.   We have to be alert and careful in all our dealings. Then only we can earn, save, and be contented with what we do. " Suresh concluded.

When the words profit, earnings, savings etc., came for discussion, Abdullah, recollected the teachings at the Masjid, during the prayers, that any business should be in accordance with the Law of Shariya and that there should not be any cheating in any business.

Abdullah got immersed in his own thoughts, that something must necessarily be done for a livelihood. Can he run the mutton shop, sincerely, honestly, as per the stipulations mentioned in Quran? Would it be possible for him? Is the decision taken, to run the mutton shop wrong, or right?

"What happened? Why don't you pay attention to my words?" Suresh questioned Abdullah.

"Yes, I am listening to you. I thought, till now, mutton shop means, only selling mutton, but there are many other matters, related to the business, which I realize only now". replied Abdullah.

"Do you think, all mutton dealers are familiar with all these intricacies? Do not think too much about it. Over a period, you will certainly learn all of them, with your experience. Should I get the chicken now? Since Rasul is also available now, he will do the *Halal* and you can start the work today itself. " Suresh advised.

"I understand, what you explain. But my mind is still full of doubts and questions. Unless they are cleared and I feel satisfied, I am not willing to start the shop", frankly declared Abdullah.

"Yes, people with delicate hearts, find it hard to run a mutton shop. Speak out your doubts and I will try to explain them," Suresh assured.

"Dear Suresh, you strongly believe in Hindu religion. Both Hindus and Muslims purchase mutton from your shop" Abdullah with an enquiring face, asked Suresh.

Suresh smiled and said, "Your father, a Muslim, when ran the mutton shop, did they, people from both religions, not buy mutton there? Rasul is the only person, who does *Halal* in both the shops, run by both Hindus and Muslims. Religion is the way of living, but not a tool for division among people. Generally, Muslims do halal in all the mutton shops, irrespective of the fact whether it is run by a Hindu or a Muslim. Then people belonging to both religions do buy mutton from both shops. In this process, both the religions are equal" Suresh explained non-stop.

"How do Hindus follow the procedure, as per their customs? Before Islam came into being, what Hindus used to do for mutton?" Abdullah enquired.

" Me too never got any such doubt. What you said is right and understandable," said Suresh.

" I really want to know, more about these and I will be happy if someone could clarify my doubts" said Abdullah.

"There is one Jatka Yogaiah, in our village and he is a senior person, said to be learned in these aspects. Should we go to him and discuss it with him?" Suresh offered.

Both of them went to the home of Jatka Yogaiah. It is a big, tiled house. He sat in the easy chair, on the verandah, smoking a cigar. He has a big mustache, silver strands, with a big kumkum sectarian mark on his forehead. A long, red thread in his neck, with a locket of goddess Kalika devi, hanging from it, is very conspicuous. With the clear wrinkles on his face, a white dhoti with a big red border, and a decorative upper garment on his left shoulder, he, in his nineties, is looking very decent, commanding high respect and honor.

Abdullah and Suresh offered their respects to the elderly gentleman.

He recognized Suresh,"Are you not the one, who runs the mutton shop? Who is this boy?" He enquired about Abdullah.

"I am the son of late Karimulla, who used to run the mutton shop" Abdullah explained.

"Oh, he is the one, that recently passed away. I heard his son is associated with *Madarsa*. Is that you?" Asking thus, Jatka Yogaiah offered them seats.

"What is that I can do for you?" enquired Yogaiah.

"We are a little hesitant to ask you" Suresh initiated slowly.

"Me and my friend have some doubts and thought you only can clarify them. Abdullah wants to run a mutton shop, but he is generally a shy and calm person, not so mingling with others, just minding his own business. He always lives in the *Madarsa*, but now, he came here, seeking help from you." Suresh explained.

"It is O.K, you can ask what you wanted to know" Yogaiah assured them, enjoying the smoke from his Cigar, in his hand.

Abdullah continued," Muslims sell mutton after doing the *Halal*. Hindus also do the same thing. How come, the same procedure in making *Halal*, is followed by the people of both the religions? But, in both the cases, only Muslims do the *Halal*. Hindu religion is very ancient, and Islam came. So, before Islam, what procedures Hindus used to follow for making Halal?"

"You study in *Madarsa*. You must have some idea about Quran and other religious customs. But this is the first time someone enquired these matters with me." Yogaiah started.

"For several generations, my family used to perform the procedure of sacrificing Billy goats . Those times, people used to perform, devotional celebrations, once in six months, to the village deities. The village head used to offer the animal to the goddess. Neem leaves garlands are placed around the neck of the animal, turmeric, and *Kumkum* are smeared on the forehead of the animal and taken to the village deity, offered coconuts and with a sharp sword, they do the *Jatka*, separating the head from the body, of the animal with just one stroke. The head of the Billy goat jumps and falls at the feet of the deity. Then pooja is done to the goddess. After the prayer, the flesh of the animal is cut. One-fourth of the meat is offered to the person who did the *Jatka*. Another quarter is given to the one who donated the animal. The rest is distributed to all the villagers, free of cost. There were no sellers of meat in the village.

During the period of my grandfather, Pothuraju, there used to be four or five billy goats, that are done *Jatka*, at a time, to the Goddess. My father Pitchaiah made me perform *Jatka* when I was just eleven years old. During my time, the village prayers used to be once in a year. If anyone wants to consume meat, the animal is brought to our home and we used to do *Jatka*. We used to get one-fourth of the total meat, for doing Jatka. Hence, our surname turned to *Jatka* and I became *Jatka* Yogaiah.

Slowly, the periodicity of doing *Jatka* came down. I became old and may be, the process of *Jatka* would end with me itself. My children are educated and went for jobs, in other cities. Sometimes, I do *Jatka*, at my home only. After me, during the prayers to the goddess, to do *Jatka*, one has to come from outside our village. As a part of *pooja*, *Jatka* continues, in the religion of Hindus. While doing *Jatka*, with just one stroke, by a very sharp sword, the head of the animal gets chopped off. The animal dies instantly without any pain at all. In the scriptures, for the Saiva cult, sacrificing animals is prohibited. But, for Veera Saivas, sacrifices are accepted.

The *Halal* is the food, legally accepted, in the Arabic styles, for the followers of Islam. Muslims do follow this sacred custom. Those, who do *Halal*, read chapter 16:115 of Quran, chanting the name of Bismillah.

The animal meant for *Halal*, should be healthy and full of life. They prefer to take such food only. If the procedures are not followed systematically, such food is not accepted by Muslims. They keep the animal in the direction of the Holy city of Mecca and then only cut its neck. That leads to the belief that all the bad blood will drain off and it will die painlessly. They drain the blood completely off the animal.

My son lives in the town. When I visit my children, in the town, I observe the notices on the bill boards, in front of the mutton shops, that it is the meat, after *Halal*, *Bismillah*, etc. In bigger shops, they hire Muslims with monthly salaries for making *Halal*. To be frank, it became very common, to do *Halal* or *Bismillah* and sell the meat without any differentiation of Hindus or Muslims. Else, the business wouldn't run well. The Hindu custom of *Jatka* is not being heard much"

Yogaiah, took a long breath of smoke with his favorite cigar. He pushed the smoke into the air, making it into beautiful rings, one after the other, coming out of his mouth. He thus explained his life time experience, beautifully and interestingly to the youngsters, who became very happy to listen, which till now, they never heard in their lives.

"We are very thankful to you, for the beautiful narration and interesting explanation coupled with your life time experiences".

Suresh and Abdullah, folded their hands, with reverence, thanked Yogaiah, and took leave of him.

"With these new informative anecdotes, what is that I can do afresh and meaningful ? Whether it is good or bad, we have been running the mutton shop from the time of our forefathers. We have to continue, the same tradition and run the mutton shop too. Whether it is *Jatka* or *Halal*, it is all one and the same, to sell mutton. Why there should be this anguish of discussion, whether it is good or bad? If the people who consume meat do not have any objection, why we, the sellers of meat should have any objection or reservation?" convincing himself, Suresh started towards his shop.

After listening to Jatka Yogaiah, new questions new doubts and new thoughts started cropping up, in the mind of Abdullah. Whether it is the procedure of *Halal* or *Jatka*, is it not, simply killing the innocent animal? How could you be so cruel towards the animals? Why such customs are not applicable to vegetarians? Even the plants and trees do have life in them.

Man consumes them as food, irrespective of vegetarian food or non-vegetarian. Several thoughts, wavering in the mind of Abdullah, started disturbing him very much. He was unable to derive proper answers and solutions for those troubling thoughts and endless questions. Is it fair to kill animals for a livelihood? Whether it is fair or unfair, as evident from the scriptures, religious customs, and prescriptions, why should I kill animals and deal with that flesh and blood? Having been associated with madarsa and the teachings therefrom and other elders, should I not distinguish between good and bad, should I lead a life, contrary to the beliefs and righteous preaching learned till now?

Abdullah was unable to convince himself and go against his conscience. His feet started moving towards *Madarsa*.

*

TIP TO SERVER

"What is this?, Did I unnecessarily come to this Star Hotel? I still feel hungry though I took a plate of *Idli* and shelled down everything in my pocket. How it would be if I fill my stomach? with just water, never to mind, whether it is hot or cold?"

The tip that I give, might be bigger than the bill itself, for me, and why should I empty all my coppers, just for the sake of nice conversation or goodies from the inmate staff?

"If it is a roadside *tiffin* center, it would certainly fill up my belly, with enough chutney, sans any tips. The hot tiffin from them will console me from the hot and sweat causing climate. There is no need to spend and lose more money in the name of a tip. The cost of the tiffin is worth a few chips and that is all, being less expensive. The street vendor will offer a little more time, that is till the next day for payment in case, we run short of coins or notes. With such lucrative advantages, we automatically and voluntarily go to the same shop, the next day too!

I was forced to come to this Star Hotel today, though I do not like it. Kotaiah borrowed four thousand rupees from me with an assurance to repay that within just four days. The four days culminated into four months yet he was not to be seen. Four thousand rupees may not be a big sum, he might not do huge works with that paltry amount, but it was my hard-earned money, which I could never afford to forego though I may not need it urgently. If the money spills from our pocket, we may not feel that bad, but, if the person who borrowed money from us did not keep up his promise to repay it, we will certainly treat it as cheating which we could never tolerate. Such small-scale cheatings lead to bigger scams and need to be nipped in the bud itself.

"Why at all, did I come to this Hotel ? Is it for taking my breakfast or to give away tips? I cannot bear the cheating of four thousand rupees now. If my wife, comes to know this transaction I cannot face her and her interrogation, but is it not cheating her?

Kotaiah did not appear till now and did not come fast. How long should I wait here? I started murmuring and folding the tissue papers and keeping them in the pant pocket. At least a part of the tip could be compensated with these tissue papers. The *idli* that I had taken was two hours back, but sitting in the air-conditioned room would have matched the cost of the *tiffin*. The tissue papers, I nabbed, would be equal to that of the tip. The comfort of sitting in the air-conditioned room could match the cost of the idly that I consumed. Now, what about the GST? The plate that held the bill was also holding some white sweet *saunth*. I took a fistful of the *saunth*, and put it in my pocket. Yes, now what I spent on this hotel is apparently compensated. This star hotel is good in its facilities and gives good comfort. But all those who come here may not be as intelligent as I am in deriving the maximum benefit. I beat all of them in doing things in a smart way.

It was too boring, to wait this long, for the friend who did not turn up. I sat on the sofa, in the reception area, where there are some English and Urdu newspapers and I checked all of them. I took a couple of selfies too, and uploaded them to the Facebook, Instagram, Newshunt, and Twitter. Some of my friends, saw them so fast and gave some likes too within no time. Why not some provision should be created to buy these appreciations and likes, so that I get more money? I suddenly remembered that there is some App which contains the pictures of old furniture posted by interested sellers, luring the prospective buyers. Similar to that, someone can sell my appreciative likes, in all the social media and get me some more money.

The friend was yet to come. I waited for a long time. I felt drowsy and closed my eyes. With comfortable cool atmosphere and controlled temperature, I felt like closing my eyes, resulting into a small nap in the sofa in the reception area itself.

"Excuse me Sir, here is the money that I took from you. I return to you all that, including the tip you made here!" With the voice of some one I woke up and opened my eyes. Someone in a full suit looking rich and attractive, with a decent look with a plate in his hand was standing before me. A beautiful envelope with an attractive design over it was peeping out from the plate, along with a hundred rupee note neatly folded along with white sweet *Saumph*. Of course, there are two notes of two thousand denominations clipped with a small slip of paper too. I did not understand what was happening. I rubbed my eyes and looked at the plate again. I took the slip and kept it in my pocket, with the intention to go through it later. I took the two currency notes of two thousand denominations and the one hundred rupees note. It appeared it was the return tip for me. Incidentally I took little more of the *Saumph* and placed it in my pocket.

The money borrowed by Kotaiah, earlier, without the knowledge of my wife, came back to me. This is neither a cheating nor a scam. I got back my *tip*, along with some saumph too. I need not curse this Star Hotel any more.

People never recognize the facilities offered by these Star Hotels. That is why, they go to the road side eateries, so innocently. I cannot wait any more for my friend. The money, on which, I lost my hopes, came back safe, making me very happy.

I started walking out of the hotel. I took out the slip from the pocket. It read," Dear Sir, I express my deep sense of gratitude, for helping me, when I needed it very much. I sincerely feel very happy to return it to you. Please accept it and the tip, as well. - Yours, Kotaiah."

The lesson I learned from Kotaiah, is to return the borrowed money, with reverence and with a tip too.

Do my plans, really follow the righteousness? I can discuss this with my wife and check the correctness of my ideas. How my wife will react to seeing the four thousand rupees in my purse? I cannot face her and her questions. So, hereafter, I should not lend any money to any one. Similarly, the unpleasant feeling of giving a huge tip would also be curtailed.

From now on, I will neither go to any Star Hotel, nor tender any lavish tip there.

From tomorrow onwards I will go to roadside eateries only. This is the beautiful lesson, I learned.

*

DOLLY THE PET

Siva was loitering in the garden of his house in a pensive mood. " What happened to you? Dear Chinna, I will get you, special biryani, be calm and be cooperative" Siva tried to console his pet dog which was behaving in an unpleasant and uncomfortable manner.

The dog was not lifting its head. Siva put his right hand on its neck and the other hand below the neck affectionately patting it. The dog was not responding. It became further stiff without any positive response.

The sounds of someone coughing heavily were heard from the verandah.

"Absolutely no other work, simply coughing all the time and irritating others" Siva felt irritated.

"Please take me to the hospital the cough is not coming to control, since last night. Sometimes blood is also coming out" the feeble voice of his father was apparently helpless.

"What is the hurry for that? Dolly needs to be taken to the doctor as it is behaving very uncomfortably since last night" Siva told impatiently. He wais not in a mood to care for the cough of his father though it was tending alarming.

"It seems you do not relish the *biryani* got through swiggy. I will take you to the veterinary doctor who will needle you and then only you will eat something" a little harshness was indicated in Siva's tone.

Siva took the car out of its parking place. The cough of his father was still disturbing but Siva was not in a mood to attend to.

Siva called "Chinna! Come Let us go to the Hospital!" and the dog mustered a little energy and jumped on to Siva. He smiled at the dog, patted him and started the car to the Veterinary Hospital.

"Dear doctor, this dog is not feeling comfortable and is not cooperating with me, since last night. It is not at all responding well and is not eating the chicken *biryani*. Please examine him and find out what happened. I am very much worried and disturbed" Siva explained.

The doctor patted the dog and assured "There is nothing to worry. Just one injection will set it right. After that, it will certainly relish the biryani, no need to worry at all." The doctor administered an injection on the thigh of the dog.

"Please Doctor, please be slow and ensure there is no pain for him" Siva closed his eyes and requested as if he himself was bearing the pain, instead of his loving dog.

" It is O.K. Fine! Now my dear Dolly, let us go to the restaurant and get a tasty *biryani*" Siva said and went to the Hotel. He got a parcel of special *biryani* and returned home.

The house was silent and father's coughing sounds were absent. Siva slowly entered the house and looked at his father on the bed. There was no movement in his father. Siva went nearer to the bed but by then his father slept permanently leaving for his heavenly abode.

Siva took the *Biryani* parcel and went to the other side to feed his pet dog.

The pet dog Dolly certainly occupied such a close and lovely place in the life of Siva more than his father who could not get enough love and attention when alive or dead.

*

BUTTONHOLES FOR DRESSES

"Come in, Khasim! Have your food" Uncle Fakir called affectionately and Khasim replied in affirmation and came inside.

Uncle Fakir gave the food plate and said "Food is warm and better have it immediately lest it becomes cool." The love and affection shown by Fakir certainly covered the loss of parents of Khasim.

"Sambar is very tasty" Khasim appreciated the food continuing the eating. In fact, Khasim did not remember how his parents looked like.

"It is O.K. Finish the food quickly, lot of work is waiting. The festival season is fast approaching and lots of shirts, half pants, blouses etc. are waiting to be stitched," said Fakir.

Khasim always wondered whether he should be content with that he is getting tasty and sumptuous food daily or should he worry that he is not yet familiar with tailoring work even after living there for such a long time. This question haunts him every day.

There is no one else to look after him other than Fakir in the whole world. But for him he would have become an orphan.

When he recollects all these thoughts, Khasim becomes very sad. Uncle taught him part of the tailoring, but he always gave him the work of making the button holes, only, and nothing else. Uncle does all the tailoring work and gives the button holes work to Khasim.

Khasim carefully observes how to take the measurements of the people for making the new dresses cutting the cloth as per measurements ironing and preserving them. All these aspects are very clearly imprinted in the mind of Khasim but unless all these ideas were put into practice how the skill in the work can be exhibited and gain the good will from the people?

Uncle prefers to give sufficient food to Khasim than to eat himself. The love and affection shown towards Khasim was very high and appreciable. Both lived in a small hut. All cooking and other related house hold work was done by the uncle without assigning any work to Khasim. Even if Khasim tries to help him by fetching drinking water sometimes, his uncle lovingly warns him to not to do such tasks. Such a lovely and affectionate way of treating Khasim as his own son makes Khasim very happy and Khasim sincerely reciprocates his love towards Fakir. Sometimes Khasim worries how to reciprocate his love to his uncle.

Theirs is the only Noor Basha family in the whole village. The villagers give them the tailoring work during the festival season only. Rest of the time they remain workless. Some of the ladies would get their blouses stitched occasionally.

Fakir crossed 70 years and his vision also became weak. Still, he musters some energy and works on the old sewing machine for making the new dresses. Sometimes he does it free of cost for some poor people.

Though Fakir had been in this tailoring profession since his childhood he could not acquire any property other than the small hut in which they live.

Even the sewing machine is very old. When someone suggests to buy a new machine, he simply laughs it off. All the ladies in the village call him Jacket Fakir affectionately.

There was no occasion when anyone could point to any defect in the work of Fakir.

Khasim often thought, "Such a skillful tailor! Why doesn't he teach me the tailoring? Why he gives only the work of button holes? If anyone suggests him to take rest because of his eye sight and pass over the tailoring work to his nephew, he simply smiles and does not reply.

"Complete fixing the buttons and hooks for these shirts and blouses!"

Fakir mentioned and gave some more dresses to Khasim. "Ever since my childhood uncle gives me only this button hole work" Khasim murmured in his mind itself despite his respect for the old man.

Khasim started stitching the button holes and suddenly screamed loudly.

"How many times, did I tell you, to be careful with the sharp needle?" Fakir yelled, took the bleeding finger of Khasim and put it into his mouth. After a little while, when the pain subsided, Khasim resumed his work.

It became dark by the time Fakir finished that day's work.

"My daughter in law came home. Can I collect her new blouse? Will you finish it and give it to me soon?" An elderly lady named Andal asked.

"Amma it is not yet completed. Khasim got hurt his finger with the sharp needle. If you can give me another half an hour of time, I will complete the work and hand it over to you" Fakir replied with an apologetic voice.

"How long you continue such hard work? Why don't teach and train, stitching, to your nephew? Andal advised Fakir. Fakir simply laughed it off without any specific reply.

Andal grew a little annoyed "How can you simply laugh it off? Don't you like and appreciate my suggestion?"

"Andal Ji! Just within six months of my marriage, Allah took away my wife. I did not remarry. When my younger sister was pregnant with Khasim in her womb, my brother-in-law also merged with Allah. As soon as Khasim was born, she also left us all. Who else is there to me except this nephew? I could not get the idea of getting him educated. Had I made him well-educated, may be, he would have been a different person with a better life. He is indeed intelligent with good grasping power of learning anything that he comes across quickly. I have been closely observing him. He may be under the impression that I taught him only the button holes' work. Though he never expresses it I know for sure that he is unhappy with me"

"As long as I am alive, who will give clothes to Khasim for stitching ? After me only he will continue his life as a tailor. Of course, he is honest and hard working. He will certainly have a better future. Even if he blames or finds fault with me, I do not mind. I do not have any other properties or valuables which I can offer to him. What I possess and what I can give to him is the only tailoring occupation. I sincerely wish he will earn a very good name and fame in his work. Rest of all, I leave for the grace of Allah!"

"Even if you are an illiterate person I am very happy that you have so much confidence in your nephew. While the times changed now where even parents are not taking enough care of their own children. It is highly appreciable to notice that you take so much care of your nephew. I am sure all in the village will certainly concur with me in this" Andal appreciated Fakir.

"Is there so much love and affection associated with the work entrusted by Fakir? I could not thoroughly understand him to date. Uncle is so great that I will certainly strive hard and emulate his sincerity and honesty in my work too. All along I was wrong and it is shameful on my part if I recollect how wrongly I opined about him. I am so sorry and my heart feels so comfortable with sincere repentance"

Khasim looked at his uncle full of gratitude and walked inside the hut. He occupied his usual seat to complete the stitching of the button holes of the new dresses that lay down there pending completion.

*

THE SKY IS HIGH

It was 12.00 Noon and the Postman rang the doorbell. Tulasi opened the door and checked who it was.

"Are you Tulasi?" the Postman enquired and said "A registered cover in your name!" Tulasi nodded but felt surprised how any registered post can come in her name.

She signed the sheet given by the postman and took the cover. She looked at it and surprised that it has come from her husband Raghu.

She wondered what was the need for sending this by post while he has been speaking to her daily. What could have happened, she wondered.

She felt disturbed ever since she collected the cover from the postman and was lost in thoughts. When to open it or whether to open it at all.

She was fully confused about what to do. She completed her bath and came to the dining table. Every day Raghu would call her at that time. Even if he does not come home, it was his routine to call her and keep scolding her.

Today there was no phone call from him. She could not telephone him and enquire. She could talk to him, only when he called her. Every day during the lunch time he would be scolding her several times and unless he permits her to eat food, she could not take it. For the last ten days Raghu was not coming home but today neither he came nor his phone call. Instead, a registered cover came to her.

Tulasi was disturbed and felt uncomfortable. She waited till 4.00 in the evening. She felt very hungry. As she is pregnant even the child in her womb added to her strain.

In such uncomfortable feelings she took some biscuits and made a cup of tea for herself. She put them on the teepoy and sat in the chair. She tried to be calm and cool. She could not venture to open the cover. She got up and moved slowly to the window on the north. She pushed the curtains of the window side ways and started looking through the window, standing still. Many vehicles were moving on the road in both the directions.

Many pedestrians too were there on the road moving in all directions. She felt as if she was seeing all those for the first time and felt a little fresh.

Should I read the letter or not? What happens if it is read? What happens if it is not read? With several thoughts and ideas, she simply stood there staring outside. She looked up to the sky and her heart opened up towards the past.

Ananda Rao's wife passed away. All the relatives advised him that he should marry again so that the girl child could be raised well. Respecting all of them he married Parvathi. He got a wife but she could not become a mother to the child Tulasi who was just 5 years old. Ever since her childhood Tulasi had been helping her step mother in the household chores.

She stopped going to the school after 7th standard. She loved her father very much but could not get the same in reciprocation. Though her step-mother Parvati had been harsh to Tulasi, she always wished her father should be happy always.

As soon as Tulasi turned 16, Parvati made several attempts to get Tulasi married and send her off the house. Ananda Rao passed away by then with ill health. Parvati was very anxious to get rid of Tulasi and got her married to Raghu a distant relative.

Even after the marriage, there was no change in the life of Tulasi. The work and responsibility increased manifold.

Raghu worked as a junior with a senior advocate. He bought a Flat before his marriage. Tulasi quickly grasped the likes and dislikes of her husband Raghu and his needs too. She molded herself to move in the way that is desired by Raghu. She dedicated her life to fulfilling the needs and necessities, likes and dislikes, tastes and temperaments of her husband.

Despite her sincere dedication and surrender of her life her husband Raghu never extended enough respect to his wife

Tulasi. Instead, he was always scolding, abusing, and hurting her sentiments which became a daily affair in her unpleasant and unsatisfactory life.

During lunch time, at the court, Raghu always, shouted at her over the phone about the food that it was less salty or saltier or on some pretext or the other. Unless he permits Tulasi could not have her food. If he came to know that Tulasi took her food, before his permission, he became violent and physically beats her very much. The body pains because of such abuses were so unbearable for her that she prefers not to have food without his consent. Even if the food in the carrier becomes cool his hot abuses over the phone were hurting much. She has been suffering these hardships and misery for the last four years.

That day Raghu came home as usual and started quarreling with Tulasi. Daily routine life also became very difficult to digest.

"What are you doing? Should you not offer hot coffee as soon as I come home?" Tulasi gave coffee to him silently and without uttering a single word but Raghu continued his shouting. She observed something strange in the words and the style of speech of Raghu.

"May be there might have been some work pressure or a problem in the court today" she convinced herself.

Suddenly he shouted, "You go out and live somewhere else. I cannot tolerate you anymore and I will divorce you"

Tulasi got a shock of her life. She could not recollect any mistake done by her for which Raghu was shouting and abusing her. She felt very unhappy and uncomfortable with the harsh words of Raghu, but she couldn't venture to reply anything to him.

"I am going out. You stay here!" Raghu took his bundles of court papers some books and went out the home. She felt severely shocked for what Raghu spoke and acted. She became speechless and simply stared at Raghu, when he was going out the home.

Raghu went to the room of a friend. He felt happy and relieved, for coming out his house staying alone peacefully and individually without having to think about Tulasi.

Since it was a holiday to the court, Raghu got up late from bed. He opened his eyes and looked at both the sides of bed in the room. He did not find Tulasi who used to offer the bed coffee to him daily as soon as he got up.

He used to curse her, "I am so unfortunate to look at your face early in the morning as a bad omen and I do not know what is going to happen to me."

Raghu remembered Tulasi in his friend's room, but no coffee came to him. He rubbed his eyes and came out of his bed, to the hall, where he saw his friend Pravin going through the newspaper and sipping his coffee.

"What is this Pravin, You could have offered coffee to me also. You know very well that I have the habit of taking bed coffee"

"you can make the coffee as per your taste, in the kitchen", Pravin replied.

Raghu did not relish the reply. His mood got spoiled. As he did not know how to make coffee, he went out with the night dress to a small tea shop on the road near their room and took a coffee. He could not like the taste and put it away after a couple of sips. He came back to the room and sat with Pravin chatting with him about his practice etc.

Pravin replied a bit pensively, "Raghu! Your advocate boss gives you a salary every month and so you are better than me. Though I started my individual practice, I am forced to wait for the cases to come. You know big cases will not reach us and I am pulling on these days somehow."

Raghu turned silent and later went to the wash room. There was no towel the soap was almost exhausted and there was no hot water in the bucket. The wash room was stinking with foul smell. He recollected Tulasi's daily words, "Here is the hot water and a towel. Please get ready, come soon and I will serve the hot breakfast."

Raghu rubbed his eyes and checked for the hot water tap. There was none. Pravin advised Raghu if at all he wants hot water he should use the stove and make it. Raghu did not appreciate the cold-water bath and somehow, he finished it and came out of the bath room, wiping his body with a towel.

He looked for the breakfast and checked with Pravin who replied that they can have the tiffin outside only.

Raghu recollected Tulasi's words, "I made hot *puries* and kept ready on the dining table. Please have it fast lest the warmth subsides." Her words were ringing in his mind, but she was not to be seen anywhere there. He dressed up and went out to a street vendor for tiffin, ordered a plate of *puries,* and got it. He tasted them but it was very salty and not at all palatable. Had it been Tulasi he would have taken her to task. But she was not there and he cannot find her. He somehow finished his plate of *puries* and came back to the room.

His advocate Ramchander telephoned Raghu and so he immediately collected the court papers and started on his bike.

He took down the dictation from the advocate and put up the relevant files. During the lunch period, the advocate reminded Raghu that some more papers were to be prepared for filing in the High Court, the next day and so Raghu should finish his lunch and attend to the important work necessary.

He remembered his words to Tulasi about the food for lunch " What is this poor cooking? Can you ever learn how to cook food and make tasty curries? You only eat it; I cannot tolerate such bad taste"

He could not see Tulasi despite his recollection of his abuses to Tulasi.

He did not feel like having food and concentrate on his work.

Meanwhile, the advocate gave some more papers to Raghu. He finished all the work for that day and came back to his room of Pravin.

"Pravin! I want to have a cup of coffee" Raghu requested.

"If you want, you can always make it. I am in the habit of having it at once, that too in the morning" Pravin replied.

Raghu started loitering in the room made the next day's court papers ready and arranged them in the required order.

Pravin was not free for any chatting. There was no TV in the room. Time was limping.

"Dear husband you had your lunch long back. You cannot bear your hunger. I am preparing the food which will be ready in another half an hour. Till that time, please have and enjoy these snacks" she used to offer a plate of some sweets and other condiments. Her words were ringing in his ears, but she was not to be seen anywhere around.

Raghu asked Pravin, "How about dinner?"

"There is no plan to cook. We will go to the mess and have it there. I usually go for dinner after 10. If you feel hungry you can go have it and come back" Pravin sounded a little indifferent.

"Dear husband I served food in a plate on dining table. Please get ready and come soon. Your favorite Pepper *Rasam* is there in the menu" Her words started ringing in his ears but Tulasi was not found anywhere.

"Nonsense! Do not pester me now. I need to make an urgent phone call" was the then reply of Raghu.

A mere silence engulfed Raghu.

He went to the mess, took a token and occupied his seat. The server served rice and vegetable curries. At the end, Raghu asked for rasam and the server brought it in a cup and smiled. It was Raghu's habit to have rasam daily with his dinner. Raghu finished dinner, and got up towards the wash basin. The person in the counter sought for the attention of Raghu to the notice board kept there where in it was painted as "Food is Virtual God. Never waste it"

Raghu got irritated. I paid money and it is my will and pleasure what to eat and how much to eat. He went to the sink, washed his hands returned back to his room. Since there was no other work Raghu lied down on the bed.

"What is this? Tulasi automatically comes to my mind every minute and in every aspect?"

He was unable to digest the fact of Tulasi occupying his each and every thought. He was unable to spend time which was moving very slowly.

Next day, when Raghu was about to start to the court, he slipped a bit and the toe of his foot got hurt and blood started oozing out.

"Dear husband! You could have been more alert. Let me apply this tincture for relief. Then, please see the doctor immediately and have the antiseptic injection so that the wound will heal up!" Tulasi's words rang in his mind.

Blood was still oozing out from the toe. Raghu held it tight with his hand for a while and the oozing stopped. Then Raghu went to the court.

Raghu, with great difficulty, dragged a week without Tulasi. He made up his mind and made a decision. But the ego was coming in the way of talking to her. He took a white paper and wrote on it in a style that came to his mind. He sent the same to her by registered post.

Tulasi mustered all her strength, slowly moved back from the window to the teepoy sat in the chair and picked up the letter. Many thoughts occupied her mind and she learnt many interesting lessons from such thoughts and experiences earlier. She heaved a sigh of relief and got back to her work. Now Tulasi was not waiting or anticipating for a phone call from her husband.

Another three days passed and the doorbell rang in the morning. Failing to guess who it could be, Tulasi opened the door to find Raghu standing there with a smile. He came inside quickly and sat in a chair.

"Don't you know to get me a hot coffee even after my arrival?" His own ever dominating and inimitable style Raghu started.

Tulasi remained silent without uttering any words. The tears that rolled down her cheeks did not understand the pain of her heart. The responses that came to stand still has no chance to touch the mind. The moment that was past always past and never returns. The ice that melted never regains its lost form. There was no meaning to this responded love showered by her which always remained as one sided.

Tulasi went inside her bed room. She took her saris and other clothes put them in a bag and came out to the hall. She never looked at Raghu and stepped out of the house. She did not reply his queries of where and why she was going and stepped out of the lift of the apartment.

Raghu could not understand what was happening and came out to the verandah. She was not found there. He quickly rushed inside the house and looked through the window on the northern side. There he saw Tulasi slowly crossing the road with her bag. He stared for some time helplessly. A little while later Tulasi was beyond his sight. He started staring at the gigantic and blue sky with no limits and no edges through the window.

*

....to be continued

CADAVER TUB

Goutham was cooking food and getting things ready for the lunch halfheartedly. Why not I make my favorite curry? Having thought so, he took some potatoes, washed and peeled them, cut into small pieces, started frying in the pan with some oil, on the gas stove.

He put rice in the pressure cooker and poured four cups of water in it, put the weight on the lid and lighted the second burner.

He mixed the potato pieces with a spoon and checked whether they were properly fried or not, by tasting one or two pieces. He was so happy with it and proud of his own cooking.

Goutham did not know how mother used to cook as she passed away in his early childhood. His father Seshaiah did not marry again. He carefully and affectionately took care of Goutham.

In several issues of his upbringing, Goutham felt very dissatisfied with his father. He could not express them to his father. The dissatisfaction slowly increased with time.

Since he did not pay proper attention to the cooker, the weight on it blew off with the steam. He put off the burner and replaced the weight on the cooker properly.

As soon as the potato curry came out as per his taste, he put off the burner, took out the curry from the frying pan placed it in another utensil, and kept it on the dining table. He went into the kitchen, transferred the rice into a bowl, and placed that also on the dining table with a lid on it.

He looked at his father on the bed. He felt happy having prepared his favorite potato curry. He felt happy, as he is going to have it and make his father also eat the same potato curry. Goutham took a towel and went to the washroom.

"Whether I like it or not, I have to eat it silently whatever is made by the father all this time." His mind was full of various thoughts some making him angry with his father. After finishing his bath, he came to the hall and looked at his father with a smile. He went to the bedroom, got dressed up, and looked in the mirror. He felt a little proud and confident combed his hair and came back to the hall.

Goutham checked his bag of books arranged the lunch box and filled his water bottle with drinking water. He served some rice and potato curry on a plate and happily consumed it. He gulped some water and finished his food. He took the plate to the sink, washed it, and kept it on the shelf. He put the lunch box and the water bottle in his bag.

He told his father "Father! I made rice and curry. I placed them on the dining table. When you get up, fresh up and then you can have it. After that you can have your tablets also. During the noon time too, you can have rice and curry. I have done whatever I could do. I am now going to college" He closed the door and started towards his college.

Venkata Seshaiah, who was lying on the bed woke up slowly, pushed the bed sheet aside, and started coughing. He took some water from the metal utensil and drank it. The cough slowly subsided.

He got down from the cot and felt very weak. He moved slowly to the washroom. He finished his morning chores and looked for his son at the dining table and confirmed that his son went to college. He slowly walked towards the dining table. He took a few tablets meant to be taken before food and drank some water.

He walked for some time in the room itself. He sat at the dining table and served himself rice on a plate. He opened the lid and checked in the second bowl where he found the potato curry in it. He closed the lid and put the bowl aside. He checked for any other items like powders etc, but could not find them. He dislikes potato curry and, could not relish it. He tried to eat alone the rice and even the rice was not soft and he found it hard to consume. As some tablets were to be taken by him, he gulped a few morsels of rice and then swallowed some more medicines. He drank some water slowly, went to his bed and sat over it.

When his wife Seethamma used to cook and serve him, he used to forget all his physical hardships of his work and his financial difficulties. Even his earnings were very low, she used to adjust with itself. When the ginning mill where he used to work was shut down for some months it was very appreciable for her how she managed the house with limited resources. She never asked for anything for herself. He used to buy a sari for all festival occasions in the year. With her sweet smile he used to fill his heart with happiness.

Though once in a while he used to shout at her, she never minds or gives a reply. She simply manages every situation with her bewitching smile.

She used to find out whatever he likes and prepared the same items. Within three years of the birth of Goutham, she passed away from cancer and ever since his bad times started.

Though some of his relatives advised and even forced him to remarry he did not do so. If he marries again, he might get a wife, but Goutham would not get a mother was his strong conviction.

Ever since Seethamma passed away Venkata Seshaiah looked after Goutham very carefully and affectionately. Even while going to duty at the spinning mill, he used to take Goutham along with him to the factory.

While Goutham grew up Venkata Seshaiah admitted him into a Government School. He put him in the social welfare hostel till his 10th class. Goutham passed his 10th class and joined College to go from his home.

Like his wife Seethamma, Seshaiah also became a good and skillful cook. He used to make several varieties of food but Goutham liked only some of them. But Seshaiah used to insist on Goutham to take those mentioning that they are good for health. He used to make Goutham study as per his ideas and convictions. But Goutham used to dislike the feelings and deeds of his father Seshaiah.

Goutham had some other plans for his higher studies but Venkata Seshaiah used to enquire several elders about the line of education preferable to which course of study would be better, and used to pressurize or push Goutham in that line of study whether he liked it or not.

Goutham preferred to study social studies but his father admitted him into biological sciences. Venkata Seshaiah wanted his son Goutham should become a doctor as there were no doctors in his family and a doctor can serve society and become a respectable person in the area.

While working in the ginning mill he used to understand the difficulties, hurdles, and inconveniences of his fellow workers and believed that the illiteracy of the people was the root cause of such social disparities. He decided that his son must be well educated that too with systematically organized life through Government schools and reside in hostels where he could get to know the different situations of life and social inequalities and mold his own life in a positive manner. Even though He did not appreciate it, Venkata Seshaiah somehow forced Gowtham to fall in line. Goutham was, no doubt, intelligent, but sometimes he was behaving foolishly or childishly which hurt Venkata Seshaiah.

Goutham was born when his father was 47 years old. With old age setting in and with the pollution in the work because of the dust, the health of Venkata Seshaiah started slowly deteriorating. Continuous work in the ginning mill spoiled both of his lungs and he was forced to retire from working further. Following the doctor's advice, he confined himself to home, using medicines and resting.

Though he did not directly participate in the activities or movements of their laborers Venkata Seshaiah acquired leadership qualities and name and fame in and around the factory. With his analytical skills and knowledge, he used to suggest solutions for various practical problems. Several important leaders wooed him to join political parties with good offers of postings but he avoided it and did not join in any political party. He maintained self discipline.

He used to paint red color to his house doors. Over time, his house was popularly known as Red Door Seshaiah in the place because of the conspicuous looks in the vicinity.

He underwent several financial hardships and problems in his life. But he wanted to make his son a successful and great personality. But as things that were going on, he felt very dissatisfied. He could not understand or realize why Goutham was so antagonistic against him. With several thoughts and memories rising in his mind, Venkata Seshaiah lay on his bed looking at the roof with a feel of helplessness.

Somehow, Goutham was showing his repulsion and disinterest in cooking the food for the last three months but Venkata Seshaiah was unable to express those feelings outside. The sorrowful feelings were more than those of losing his wife. He was unable to get what was the real crux of the problem with Goutham. If it was clear he would have taken some correcting steps. Since Venkata Seshaiah was getting weak with bad health, he was unable to attend any work and had to confine himself to the home. Various memories, thoughts and ideas made a severe whirlwind in his mind making him suffocated and helpless.

After the death of his wife, he never expressed his anger over his son.

It was lunch time and Venkata Seshaiah picked up some stamina to go to the dining table. The same rice which was not cooked completely was collected by him on plate. He took a few morsels of the food forcibly and later took a few medicines with a glass of water. Coughing a little he stepped towards his bed.

There was a heavy breeze and the doors opened. Venkata Seshaiah went near the door and looked at them affectionately. The red colored paint of the doors gave him good energy and satisfaction. He closed the doors and moved back to his cot with a smile on his lips.

Time appeared to move very slowly and without his knowledge and involvement. He wanted Goutham to be a doctor. It might not be possible to see him as a doctor at present as he thought that he would not survive for a long period.

There was a big and repeated knock on the doors. Seshaiah got up with the loud noise slowly from his bed and opened the doors.

"I thought of not disturbing and troubling you and so I closed the doors without bolting. I went to the College. But you are doing like this now bolting from inside!" Goutham came inside and expressed his unpleasant feelings.

He kept his bag in the chair, took the lunch box to the sink in the kitchen, and cleaned and washed it.

"Every student is blaming this College for poor performance of the students. I have to bear and tolerate it bowing my head with insult. If there are no necessasary facilities in the very first year itself, how can I come up in my studies here? There is a library but no sufficient books. It is less said the better to speak about the ill-equipped laboratories. Sufficient corpses are not available for the anatomy classes and so the practical classes are going only for name's sake without thorough practicals for the last four years, dissecting the same dead body again and again. The disappointment and dissatisfaction are on the rise for the last few years. Had I joined BA, I could have read the books and gotten good marks. Instead, I am now in MBBS as per the wish of the great Venkata Seshaiah that I should become a doctor at any cost irrespective of my taste, level of interest and the competency"

Expressing these, Goutham came near the dining table, checked the utensils there on and found that a little rice seems to have been consumed but the potato curry remained intact and untouched.

"I took much trouble and prepared this food but he seems to be not recognizing my style of cooking. He does not like the food made by me. Why he does not love me and without consuming food how can he survive?" Goutham became restless and impatient.

Goutham cleaned all utensils and arranged in the kitchen, came to the hall.

"Father! You need to take some tablets I will go to the shop and get you some bread." Saying so, Goutham brought the bread and kept it on the stool beside his bed along with a glass of water.

"Take the bread and then have the tablets. I have lot of work to do" Goutham went to his room.

As usual, Goutham got up early in the next morning. He came to the hall and put on the light. He looked at his father. A paper kept on the stool was waving with the breeze of the fan. He took off the water glass and took the paper and read it.

He looked at his father and checked his pulse. He was not getting the pulse. He widened the eyes and checked. They were not moving checked heartbeat it was totally silent. Goutham understood that his father was no more. The feelings totally stopped in Goutham. He took two ice cubes from the fridge rolled in two hand kerchiefs and placed at the eyes of his father. He informed the Jeevanandan team which reached within 30 mts. They collected the eyes and took away the dead body of Venkata Seshaiah. Goutham did not go along with them but stayed back at home. Somehow, the guilty feelings were not getting off about his father.

The garland of plastic flowers placed on the picture of Venkata Seshaiah was slowly moving as if something was to be whispered to Goutham. He slowly turned to the side ways.

He was attending the College and returning back without the sadness that his father left for the heavenly abode.

It was the nature's characteristic to move on without waiting or caring for anything or anyone. Four months passed off. If the time takes revenge even a beautiful music tune may turn out to be a sorrowful cry. The strong memories are not shaken so easily. With more and more time, may be the anger revenge and guilty feeling might subside.

He made his favorite dishes put it in the lunch box and he locked the house and went to the college.

Anatomy lesson was scheduled on that day. But what was there to learn? Goutham satyed in canteen. After a while, his mobile phone rang. It was Ashok calling. Goutham answered the phone call.

"Where are you, Goutham? Today you have not attended the Lab. Assistant professor enquired your presence to the anatomy practicals. We are anxiously waiting for you. Please come soon"

Ashok explained everything to Goutham.

"It is O.K. I will join lab soon. I am in canteen" Goutham put off the phone took his bag and reached the lab.

All his friends rained queries why Goutham was late that day unlike his daily punctual presence.

"No no, there is nothing special worth mentioning. I simply sat in the Canteen presuming that there may not be any new lesson to learn," replied Goutham.

Meanwhile the Assistant Professor Brahma Reddy came to the Lab and reached his table. All the six medical students of the batch surrounded the table.

Two attenders came there and took out the corpse from the tub holding the legs and shoulders and placed it on the table.

"Dear medicos! This person donated his eyes after his death. He donated body to our college. Since long we could not do the practical of anatomy perfectly as we could not get a body for it. Since we got this body, the situation changed for the better. Let us utilize this opportunity well. We will learn the anatomy of chest and the heart today. Dear Goutham! I know you are not feeling comfortable. Start the practical work yourself" With this the Asst. Professor handed over the scalpel to Goutham.

Goutham took the scalpel and looked at the corpse. Since the eyes were removed, it was like two pot holes there. It gave a feeling that the eye pits were looking towards Goutham. He kept the scalpel at 3 inches from the heart but his hands were shivering. He could not identify his father's body till then. He was taken aback. All his hatred towards his father insulting him, etc., were reeling before him. For his better future and for the benefit of the society at large, why he wanted him to become a doctor was slowly getting realized.

Would the feelings and ideas of those laborers who carried the red flags be so realistic and pragmatic? Without a proper education, how could one study the society and teach lessons to the medicos for larger wellbeing of the society? Parents might not be well educated but their strong positive vision for a better society was beyond anyone's imagination. Goutham started realizing various aspects. He looked at the Cadaver Tub. The movements like waves of the chemicals and the liquids in it were indicating and teaching him new lessons life. The holes at the place of the eyes were showing him a new way of life. Each and every part of the body was ready to offer to teach various lessons of life to him.

The change brought by the time created several turns and modes in Goutham's outlook. His heart was filled with the ideology that the welfare of the society was the ultimate aim of the medicine and the medical treatment. The changes in the ideology brought by the powerful time turned the life of Goutham, his ideas and the plans. The ultimate goal of the medical treatment to be done by him was only for the welfare of the society for the individual benefit of the people of the society. His heart was flooded with plans of making the people healthy and bereft of deceases and ailments.

With an apron of shining white on the body, with a stethoscope tossed in the hands with a smile on the bright faces was the common and natural scene at the entrances of the medical college. Their sight indicates that the powerful medical army fully equipped to eradicate all the physical ailments and inconveniences in humanity is ever ready to face and effectively deal with the eventualities and create a healthy society. This willpower was very strong fulfilling the aims of the education and confidently stepping ahead and it was very scintillating to watch and observe.

If human thoughts ideas and behavior need to turn towards progress some unforeseen incidents must take place. Just the proper education might not be sufficient to change a man. It might be partially true but may not be fully correct.

There were many examples where the lessons and realizations of the people become the root causes of the everlasting changes in the ideologies and the behavioral patterns.

The name board ws "Venkata Seshaiah Clinic." It was popular as the Red Door Hospital in the town.

That house was the same old one. Father constructed it with his honest earnings. The house was now changed into a Clinic because of Dr Goutham. The red color of the doors fills the lively activity and enthusiasm in Goutham when he looks at it. The red color always is inspiring and motivates Goutham to extend the proper systematic and courteous treatment to all those patients that visit the Clinic with several types of ailments.

Dr Goutham started a new practice of visiting the patients where they sit or wait in the clinic, testing and treating them. The treatment without any outpatient section without sending any one to the Laboratories for several tests and examinations observing the patient from all the sides and medical points of view then deciding the nature of the ailment and then prescribing suitable medicines that too inexpensive generic medicines with an affordable price, the Red Doors Hospital became familiar and popular among all the surrounding inhabitants very fast. He arranged blood freely to the needy patients whenever it was needed and this brought popularity, name, and fame to Dr Goutham. He himself donates blood at least four times in a year. His act inspires the local youth to donate blood throughout the year. Because of such continuous and uninterrupted blood supplies to the needy patients, Dr Goutham was loved, appreciated and respected by one and all there.

On a suggestion by some of the patients, he arranged a donation box for supporting the clinic financially. No display boards like "Please help us, you can put your donations here" etc., were there, except an open box without a lock placed in the verandah of the clinic. Not only the patients who got the treatment there but also outsiders and others used to place some money in the box.

With such money, the generic medicines the chemicals for the various tests, and salaries for the nurses and other employees were managed. Dr Goutham never looked into the accounts of the donation box. He simply ordered those medicines and chemicals from the market. Some donors and philanthropists used to buy some medicines and give them to the clinic free of cost for helping the patients.

Every day at least fifty persons used to get medical services from the clinic. The government also recognized the quality service rendered by Dr Goutham. They offered him an award at the state level but he did not accept it. Sometimes, he himself wonders about the medical services offered by him. He remained a bachelor, as he felt, the marriage may be an impediment to his service to the needy patients.

The inspiration and the motivation from the red-coloured doors make him happy and contended. Sometimes, he forgets his father as his picture was placed on the wall behind his regular seat. He felt very happy and truthful in fulfilling his father's ideologies and wishes in treating the patients which gives him an enormous sense of fulfillment.

"You may have to go to the city and get examined there since we do not have those special facilities here"

Goutham examined a patient and suggested to him.

"Sure Doctor, I will do it." The patient got up replied with folded hands and left.

Goutham took pity on that patient who was a young lad of just 17 appearing to be a smart and intelligent one. He lost both his parents very early. His name was Siddharth studying second year intermediate class in a Government Residential College. Goutham looked at Siddharth going out and got busy in examining another patient. It is a little delayed that day as there are many number of patients to see.

Goutham went inside the kitchen. He remembered his father when he saw the potatoes and there are tears in his eyes instantly and automatically. He kept the potatoes aside and thought of making Dal curry. He put some red gram, some water, some pieces of onions along with other ingredients in the cooker, placed the lid on it and lighted the burner with a lighter. He came back to the clinic and sat in the chair. He started slowly rocking in the chair.

He saw the picture of his father late Venkata Seshaiah and immediately became emotional. Though his father passed away, ten years back it was as if he was moving before him. Gowtham did not think of his father while examining the patients. But he always feels that the red color of the doors of the clinic always inspires and guides his course of life.

If he thinks or imagines about how a man turns after his death Goutham gets perplexed. During a life time, one may be selfish and lead a life with hatred and at a very low standard of life.

The desires were so dominating that people spend their whole lives in making efforts to fulfill those desires. If the money or the financial resources were not enough, they borrow money from others to reach their goals of desires.

For good food, health, luxurious living etc., people run after them as if they live only for the sake of impressive living. Once the life goes off, the body becomes a corpse. Relatives, friends and family members cry for the separation of the dead ones and express their sorrow and condolences. Then, either they burn the body or cremate it in the land. The life comes to an end with such a burial.

If the ideas thoughts and feelings that one had to be helpful even after death were to be inculcated there was no need for higher education, wealth or any teachers. If one thinks on the righteous lines, he can know how to be useful to society, even after one's death. There was no life after the death. But did anyone get the noble ideas or feelings that the body after death could be useful to the society? How many were getting such ideas and how many were putting them into practice?

Whenever Goutham looks at the picture of his father Venkata Seshaiah a silent message wakes him up, alerts him and creates a new awareness in his mind.

With all those heavy and serious thoughts, Goutham forgot the time but the whistles of the cooker reminded him and brought him back to the normal life and the time.

He put off the burner and put the cooker down from the gas burner. He finished cooking the Dal too. He took a plate and served himself some food came to the dining table and finished his lunch with the beautiful reminiscences of his life.

He went to the bed room and lay down on the bed and immersed in his memories and thoughts.

Though he earned a lot of name and fame, Dr Goutham always preferred to lead a very simple life. He smiled simply about how he acquired all those noble qualities for a simple life.

The clinic was booming with patients and related activities even at 6.00 PM. Goutham got ready himself and visited all the patients, examined and prescribed the necessary medicines by 11.00 PM to complete all the patients for that day.

There was no holiday for the clinic. Attending the patients on all the days in the week brought very high respect and fame to Goutham in the locality.

Dr Goutham became more popular among the general public than his father Late Sri Venkata Seshaiah. His ambition was only to extend better medical help to more and more people while all his plans' ideas and discussions go in that direction only. Such thoughts make him sometimes very dissatisfied.

With more plans of Dr Goutham to improve his medical services to people, some voluntary organizations offered to honor him in the public avenues so that his great services got recognized by one and all but Goutham pushed aside all such offers subtly.

"When I see the reports, I feel that your both kidneys are not functioning up to their full capacity. You may have to change at least one of your kidneys" Goutham expressed his concern while he examined the reports brought by Siddharth.

Siddharth felt very painful and lost his consciousness. Water was sprinkled on him and he was made comfortable on the bed by a nurse.

A little while later Siddharth opened his eyes. It was his long-cherished dream to become a doctor and serve the society, but without realizing his dreams how his life can come to an end and this thought makes him loose his heart and painful.

He does not have enough money to go for a kidney transplantation. There are no relatives who can come to his rescue and assist. Life so far was spent in the Government Hostel only. First year intermediate course was completed. Teachers encouraged him as he was a good and bright student to go for medical course and get a good name to the college.

Recollecting about his unhealthy condition of his body health and his helplessness Siddharth started crying uncontrollably.

"Do not worry Siddharth. There is no doctor better than Dr Goutham. He would certainly treat you and cure you" The nurse consoled Siddharth. Looking at his bleak future Siddharth was very sad and started looking blank.

"Your surgery is successful. We will discharge you within a week from now"

Doctor made Siddharth comfortable in ICU. Siddharth was yet to get back fully to his senses but listened to the doctor.

It was simply miraculous and unbelievable. Despite no hope for his life and no efforts made by him to get the treatment, it was very surprising that some donor gave a kidney which was transplanted into his body. Is it not a miracle that without even knowing who was that God sent donor who restored his life Siddharth was very anxious to know. Though Siddharth could not speak clearly his signals to the doctor made his mind clear to the doctor.

"Dr Goutham donated one of his kidneys to you. He was in another ward in this hospital. We were going to discharge him today.

"With these words from the doctor Siddharth's heart was filled with gratitude towards Dr Goutham. He wanted to lift his hands to offer his salutes but the various tubes and pipes attached to his body as a part of the surgery prevented him to do so. Just with a smile Siddharth expressed his sincere gratitude.

"Doctor was likely to come out from the hospital today. How come he came forward to donate a kidney to a totally stranger patient? If he loses one kidney, how he can remain healthy and treat the other patients regularly and comfortably for long?"

The patients who came there to the hospital were all discussing about the doctor only. Since the doctor was not available for the previous ten days only the nurses are dressing the wounds making the bandages giving the injections etc. All other medical services were suspended.

Everyone was surprised when Dr Goutham arrived at the clinic by an auto rickshaw. All the people there lauded the helping attitude, service-oriented approach, soft behavior and the utmost simplicity of Dr Goutham.

Dr Goutham became immediately busy with his routine work of examining the patients daily routine services treatment advices distributing the medicines etc. Everyone was surprised to find Dr Goutham who was working with more vigor and confidence.

Time went on. Siddharth got a free seat in the Medical College and Dr Goutham also felt happy about it. He believed that Siddharth also would become a doctor and will offer his devoted and selfless services to the poor and the downtrodden.

Siddharth completed his medical course and settled as Government Doctor. Days went on covering months and years and about 20 years passed.

Siddharth became an expert Civil Surgeon and used to visit Dr Goutham periodically and their devoted relationship towards the poor and the needy flourished well.

Siddharth as a Civil Surgeon became very famous in the Government Hospital and also as an ideal citizen in the eyes of other colleagues and doctors.

Dr Goutham one day as usual came to the patients as a part of his daily routine but suddenly collapsed. The nurse standing nearby called for an ambulance and took him to the Government Hospital immediately but Dr Goutham breathed his last by then.

The nurses working in the Clinic of Dr Goutham conveyed his last wishes to the authorities. As per that his both eyes were removed and preserved for donation. The dead body was sent to the Medical College where Dr Goutham studied.

A few days later Siddharth resigned to the job and took over Venkata Seshaiah Clinic so that the medical services from the clinic went on uninterrupted.

When he entered the clinic enthusiastically the red doors of the Clinic remind his social responsibilities. He touched those Red Doors with reverence and then entered the clinic.

Siddharth strived hard in following the latest techniques in quality and improved medical services to the society even better than in the past.

Like Dr Goutham who remained celebate and made his daily routine work as a single person Dr Siddharth too followed the suit and preferred to remain celibate

The corpse of Dr Goutham with the eyes removed was waiting for medical students in the Cadaver Tub. It was waiting for the surgical scalpel to be placed on the heart to teach the medical and surgical lessons to the anatomy students.

…to be continued

*

SINDURAM

The sacred marriage function is going on with lot of fanfare. Purohit was chanting the appropriate hymns, *Slokas* and *Mantras*, systematically and loudly.

The three holy knots were perfectly tied and the *Akshatas* were pouring on the new couple.

She bent her head and held the holy Mangala Sootra with her right hand. She did not feel excited even when the holy Cumin and Jaggery paste was placed on her head and no scintillating feelings cropped up.

Purohit continued the process and the friends and relatives did not inspire any goosebumps or sweet feelings. When the silver rings were placed on the toes of her feet, when the gold ring was placed in a water vessel and she was asked to compete with the husband to take it out first, no golden shakes and shiverings arose in her. No excitement while pushing his hand and in grabbing the ring from the pot.

When the husband smoothly pressed her right foot or when the edge portion of her sari was tied to the end of his silver dhoti no happiness was generated.

Even in the game of throwing the flower - balls, there was no exciting feeling or happiness felt.

When the highly respected Arundhati star was shown in the sky, there was no enthusiasm or interest in her mind.

Even after all the different steps of the holy marriage celebration are systematically executed supported by the relatives, the feeling of fulfilment was not generated in her.

There was an auspicious time ahead and if even that programme was completed during that auspicious *lagnam* the function will be complete in all respects the Pandit mentioned.

"Madam here is your coffee. It is already delayed please have the coffee lest it will lose its warmth and the taste" attender tried to divert the attention of Madhavi from her continuous thoughts to present times.

"It is fine Suresh" Madhavi took coffee cup and started sipping it slowly. She started smiling to herself. If there was no feeling worth mentioning in the festive and one and only occasion of the marriage celebration, why there should be this event of marriage? What for this married life? If there was no pleasure even in the dreams, would there be happiness and pleasant time in the actual event of marriage?

With the never-ending chain of thoughts, she finished her coffee and kept the cup aside.

"Madam! I have been observing you that your attention is always somewhere else. Are your parents looking for any marriage proposals to you? " Suresh continued his enquiries with Madhavi.   "It is nothing like that. It would be better if you confine yourself to your work" Madhavi replied with a smile.

Since Madhavi grew up at her maternal grandmother's place, she was familiar with devotion, family customs, and cultural discourses of some learned elders etc. which thoroughly impressed her.

Though she was working in software, her heart and soul were filled with devotional feelings and spiritual thoughts.

Several spiritual thoughts and ideas always surround her heart and mind. Those aspects and thoughts give her immense happiness.

She felt happy and contended for getting spiritual and devotional feelings from her grandmother.

Some of the relatives advised their near and dear to take Madhavi as a role model and this gives her a little feeling of pride.

When her aunt advised her daughter to look up to Madhavi for her behavior and attire as a fine mature and acceptable example, how cultured she looks and how nicely she manages her work how traditional she looks, her nature of not criticizing any, Madhavi felt happy.

The beliefs and ideas of Madhavi never embarrass others. Hence relatives and friends appreciated them and took her as an ideal role model.

She was selected as the best employee in her office a number of times. All other staff appreciate her and laud her for her traditional looks and decent behavior coupled with a friendly attitude which make Madhavi happy.

But of late some dissatisfaction was creeping in her mind. She could not assign any reason for it. When the attender Suresh too asked her, she was again lost in her thoughts.

Her mother was reminding her father, very often, that Madhavi should be gotten married to a suitable boy from a respectable and traditional family. Her father nodded for it and mentioned whether she has any love for anyone in the office. Her mother did not like that and expressed her displeasure for such enquiry. How traditional and well behaved is Madhavi, and how could he say such words about her dear daughter! She could not even tolerate such words about Madhavi from her father. When Madhavi listened to all this, she became more and more happy and proud.

She was filled with thoughts and office work looks incomplete. She took permission and left office, reached home a little earlier than her regular routine timings.

Mother was surprised for this early arrival of Madhavi and enquired whether her health was good. Madhavi did not reply, but went inside the bed room and lied down on her bed.

Her mother went into the kitchen to fetch some Green Tea to her.

Venkata Seshamma told her husband that her brother informed on telephone about the ill health of her mother.

"It is O.K. You can go and visit her. I have inspection in my office for another couple of days needing my presence here.

After making some adjustments, I too will start and reach you there" replied her husband Venkatachari.

Madhavi went to the office and she felt unpleasant "If I do not take her along with me. My mother likes Madhavi very much and is affectionate to her. I will inform Madhavi and both of us will start to my mother's place"

She discussed with her husband and then informed Madhavi about their latest position.

"Amma, Seshu! I may not live for long. My days are numbered" the old lady mentioned to Venkata Seshamma in a low and feeble voice. She also enquired where Madhavi is.

"Madhavi, Come! Close. Grandmother wants to see you!" Seshamma called.

"Yes, Mom! I never thought I would see grandmother in such a precarious state of health."

Madhavi came close to her grandmother wiping her tears with her hand.

"What is this Grandmother? Is Lord Vishnu Murthy calling you? Request him to wait for a few days more." When Madhavi tried to make the situation light there appeared a glow and a smile on the face of her grandmother.

"Yes, Madhavi! As you suggested, I will request the Almighty, to allow me to attend to the granddaughter's function of marriage and till then, not to settle my accounts of life. Dear Venkata Seshamma! Are you searching for alliances to Madhavi?" she questioned her daughter.

" Yes, Mother! Once your health becomes right and you recover, you too can fix the marriage of Madhavi" Seshamma entrusted the responsibility to her mother.

Madhavi understood the health position of her grandmother.

"Grandma, What is the hurry for my marriage now? I will certainly marry a good boy selected and fixed by you" Madhavi gave assurance to her grandmother for which she smiled at Madhavi in return.

"Dear Madhavi grandmother appears to be good and fine. Shall we start back home as your father would not be inconvenienced because of our absence?"

"Mother! I wish to spend a few days more with my grandmother and take care of her." Venkata Seshamma agreed for it but in the next moment, Venkatachari stepped in enquiring about his mother-in-law.

"How are you dear Son in law? Don't you wish to perform Madhavi's marriage before I close my eyes forever?" Old lady asked to Venkatachari.

"How can I supersede your wish when you are so affectionate and loving to all of us in this matter?" Venkatachari paid his respects to his mother-in-law.

Venkata Seshamma suggested her husband that it was better to take her mother to their home for a better treatment and care.

The elderly lady smiled and told, "I have no desire to live longer. I just want to see Madhavi's marriage and then reach the heavenly abode" with a little stammer in her tone.

"How can we get a suitable alliance to Madhavi at such a short notice?" Venkatachari expressed his practical difficulty.

The elderly lady expressed, "Dear all! I had kept in my mind long back about a boy for Madhavi. Would you perform the marriage now?"

"If you select a boy, what else would be a higher blessing for us ?" Seshamma and Venkatachari uttered gratefully and Madhavi blushed with a smile on her face.

"Obliging grandmother is the ultimate in life" thinking that way, Madhavi stepped out into the verandah.

Madhavi draped herself in an ancestral silk sari, used by her grandmother in her marriage function years back and moved to her grandmother. The old lady signaled to go close to her with her right hand. Madhavi held her sari tucking and moved to close the grandmother.

"He is the bridegroom", grandmother signaled with her index finger, but Madhavi did not look up out of shyness.

Venkata Seshamma and Venkatachari accompanied Madhavi towards the old lady. The grandmother picked up some breath and signaled towards the groom but even then Madhavi could not venture to lift her head.

A cool palm touched the top of the head of Madhavi, which created an indescribable feeling with goosebumps.

The sinduram was very auspicious to wear on the forehead and the head indicating the prowess of *Sati* and *Parvati*. The bright red color will bless all the various riches to the women while safeguarding the family welfare and the children. The mark of Sinduram on the forehead was an example of the power of the woman. There lies the third eye and it was the powerful center of all the nerves in her body. It was the central point focussing all the feelings and experiences. It gives a cool feeling to that place.

The auspicious mark on the forehead not only creates the spiritual feelings but also protects from the bad and inauspicious elements which is firmly believed by one and all.

The reflections by the touch of the groom took Madhavi to a different and beautiful plane.

She was experiencing an altogether different experience, that never happened and was experienced earlier.

Madhavi was getting drenched in the rain of scintillating and positive vibrations.

Madhavi slowly turned towards her grandmother. There was a great happiness explicit on her divine face. Madhavi slowly touched the divine feet of her grandmother.

But by then the old lady merged in the eternal and divine lotus feet.

The sweet and scintillating experience was enormous and sufficient to her entire life. The moment of grandmother's journey towards God, became the auspicious moment for marriage. The Sinduram that was missing in the wedding function seen by Madhavi in her dream is presented now by the grandmother making Madhavi's life extremely happy and successful with a great sense of fulfilment.

*

THE WAVES

"Hey, What were you barking last night? Useless fellow! Just shut up your mouth and keep quiet. What do you think about me? Be careful and keep low without any noise in my house. Do you think your father bought me for millions and millions?" Neelambaram was shouting at the pitch of his voice.

Anitha, his wife replied, "Please wait for the coffee that I will bring in a moment. After having the coffee, you can leisurely shout at me".

He almost snatched the cup of coffee from her hands and sheepishly looked at his wife.

All these became very much routine and common in her life making her used for them.

She could not bear the difficulties of the poverty of her father. Her mother passed away when she was just born. Her father looked after Anitha both as her mother and father. Though the relatives suggested, he did not marry again but brought up Anitha without letting her be aware of the absence of her mother.

Though she was a good student in her school, her father could not afford to educate her beyond the 10th class in the school. He identified one Neelambaram from his distant relatives and got Anitha married to him.

Since Anitha was quite a beautiful girl despite poor educational levels he married her without any dowry.

Anitha's father always minds only the welfare of Anitha. She was the entire world to him. Working hard as a daily wager without spending anything for himself for the last four years after her marriage regularly he brings rice, vegetables, fruits, and groceries to her. Though she prevented him to do so, he gives some cash also for her daily needs to her to run the family and lead a comfortable life.

Neelambaram never behaves nicely with his wife. Whenever her father comes home Neelambaram shouts and quarrels with his father-in-law without giving him any respect whatsoever. He tortures his wife Anitha both physically and mentally. She was patient and silent in bearing all those tortures. Her intention was not to spoil the confidence her father had in her about her confidence and her ability in leading a happy life.

Neelambaram started drinking alcohol for two years. It has become his regular habit to beat Anitha and she started bearing all these very calmly.

She did not want her father to know about the unruly behavior of her husband which could make him sad and so she was bearing all these matters and inconveniences silently ever since her marriage.

"Amma! Anitha" She came out of her deep thoughts with the voice of her father. She invited him into the house.

"How is my son in law?" Seethayya enquired with a low voice.

"You must be tired of your journey. Please take this butter milk" she gave a glass of butter milk to her father.

"Is that your father?" Neelambaram shouted from the bedroom.

"Yes that is he" Anitha replied politely" Please come to the hall. My father came here. You both please keep talking and I will serve breakfast to both of you!" Anitha mentioned.

"Yes, serve him first. He might be hungry for many days together. Even his wife is also not there and so who else will feed him?" Neelambaram in a high pitch shouted and came into the hall.

"How are you, son in law?" Seethaiah courteously initiated the conversation.

Neelambaram replied harshly and scolded for his coming to his home and getting all the attention.

Anitha signaled to her husband and gave the tiffin plates to him and her father.

"Please have it!" Seethaiah respected his son in law pointing to the tiffin plate.

"Ya, I know. I will have it" Neelambaram replied a little harshly and started eating.

As soon as he took a morsel, he coughed a little.

"Do not worry, May be someone is thinking and remembering you" Anitha consoled and slowly patted on his back.

"Please eat slowly. Have some water. The uneasiness will subside", Anitha made him drink some water.

The coughing subsided.

"Please have it slowly" Seethaiah affectionately told his Son in law.

Neelambaram as usual, did not care Seethaiah or his words.

"I know it!"

Seethaiah observed Neelambaram to cough more and told, "Anitha he is still coughing. Please get some cough syrup and give it to him"

He pacified Neelambaram, not to worry as Anitha would give him some cough syrup which would make him comfortable.

"Amma, please take care of his health. I will leave now for the village" and gave Anitha an envelope. Anitha suggested him to have lunch and then to leave for the village, but he insisted on leaving.

"No, I have to leave now. I have some work there to attend. So please convey my good wishes to your husband" Saying so Seethaiah collected his bag and started to go from there.

"Fine father! Please take care of your health!" Anitha saw him off. Even after 4 days Neelambaram did not stop coughing. Anitha suggested him to go to the hospital.

But Neelambaram in his rash style refused and told, "I am not a patient and I am alright"

***

"Please take this patient to room number 4. There is a doctor and he will examine him"

The nurse advised and Anitha took her husband there.

"Please let him be seated here. What is the problem?" Doctor questioned.

"Doctor! My husband is continuously coughing since morning and the medicines that I gave for a relief did not help him" replied Anitha.

"It is O.K. Let him lay on the bed" The doctor advised and began to examine with his stethoscope.

"Are there any bad habits, was there the cough earlier too?" doctor examined and prescribed some tests and advised her to get those tests done.

She took her husband quickly to the Laboratory even while Neelambaram continued murmuring.

The technicians took an X- Ray and took the blood samples for testing. It was noon and she brought some food to her husband and served him affectionately. Neelambaram continued his murmuring and unpleasantness.

Anitha collected all the reports from the Lab and saw the doctor with the reports.

"Amma! The patient's position is alarming. His liver got spoiled. If you admit him into the hospital, surgery needs to be done to him urgently. Is there anyone who can donate a liver to him? Doctor mentioned.

"I am his wife and I will donate my liver to him and kindly make the necessary arrangements for the surgery" Anitha replied instantly.

"It is nice. You get admitted into the hospital. We will verify whether your liver is suitable for him or not" the doctor advised.

Anitha felt uneasy and thought she could have requested her father to be with her.

"Surgery is successful. There is no danger to your

husband's life. You brought him to the hospital in the right time"

Doctor came out of the operation theatre and pacified Anitha when he said that her lever does not match her husband's lever. She felt very unhappy.

"You can go inside and see the patient", Doctor announced but she felt very uncomfortable to go inside and look at her husband. Though she nodded affirmatively she could not venture to go inside.

Neelambaram came out of sedation and slowly tried to open his eyes. No one was near to him. He looked for Anitha, but could not find her.

"Sir you have to take rest and do not move or exert much. The person who donated the liver to you is on the bed next to you" The nurse told him.

Neelambaram looked to his left and was surprised. It was Seethaiah and was looking at Neelambaram with a happy smile on his face.

Tears rolled over the eyes of Neelambaram. Though he had been shouting, abusing, and insulting with no respect for himhe, in spite of all these donated his liver giving a new lease life to Neelambaram.

He felt ashamed for his unruly behavior towards his father-in-law.

His eyes were full of repentance and guilt looking at Seethaiah apologetically and reverentially.

The wave of love and affection evident in the looks and eyes of Seethaiah wiped out the anger and hatred of Neelambaram. Neelambaram folded his both the hands gratefully and respectfully offering his salutes to Seethaiah unintentionally and automatically. The craving request for pardon was felt whole heartedly and the indescribable expressions by Neelambaram slowly moved towards Seethaiah which Seethaiah passionately understood.

*

LOTUS FEET OF HUSBAND

"Come on! Get ready fast. It is time for my duty" Venkata Swamy hurried his wife.

"It is almost over. Just ten minutes more!" patiently replied Venkata Ramana to her husband.

"Go ahead. Venkata Swamy checked himself in the mirror and adjusted his police cap on his head.

"Here it is. I kept *Paayasam* in the can, *Chakkera Pongali* in the box, *Pulihora* in another box and all these in the carry bag. I did all those what you advised. Will all our difficulties be cleared at least from now?" Venkata Ramana enquired with her husband.

"Do not worry my dear ! Trust me!" he assured.

"I sincerely trusted you for the last 25 years. You can start now, before *Raahu Kaalam* begins" she accompanied him for a few steps.

She came out and returned in the opposite direction as an auspicious omen for the success of his efforts.

Venkata Swamy smiled, put his lunch bag on the bike and started for duty. He was very happy. He was visualizing ahead, beautiful solutions for all the problems and difficulties of his life. He felt as if he was dancing in the skies and not running on the bike.

He came very fast to the station, unlike his daily journey of half an hour. He collected his bag and entered the station.

Except the night guards, none has reported yet for the duties. He reached his seat, sat, and kept his bag on the table. After signing the attendance register, he took his bag and walked towards the lock-up room.

He stood before the lock-up room, saw through the iron grills, and folded his hands.

"Amma ! My wife got up very early morning before sunrise took her bath and then prepared this *Prasadam* very fresh. Kindly accept this and bless this devotee!" he humbly requested her who was inside.

Amma who sat on a cement slab inside the lock up room slowly lifted her head, looked at Venkata Swamy, and smiled at him.

Venkata Swamy became cheerful and folded his hands once again and he put the bag inside the lock up room through the iron bars of the grill door.

She looked at him affirmatively and became silent.

"I am blessed. Thank you Amma!"

He folded his hands again and offered his salutations to her. He came back to his seat and sat there.

Even while on duty the attention of Venkata Swamy was on her only. He was hopeful that the appropriate time has come for him when all his desires and aspirations would fulfill.

All the other police staff started reaching there one after the other. As and when time passed, he felt the urge to go to her once again. He got up from his seat and walked towards the lock up room. He became very thrilled finding that she consumed the *Prasadam* brought by him.

As soon as she finished consuming, she put all the boxes in the bag and came near the door.

"Amma ! Please bless me!" Venkata Swamy prostrated before her.

"I want my daughter's marriage to be performed and my son aspires for a Government Job" he slowly murmured while praying to her.

Venkata Swamy suddenly felt a touch and lifted his head to find Murali the court constable. He signaled Venkata Swamy to move aside.

From the lock up room Amma looked calm and cool and looked at Venkata Swamy pleasantly. He saw her gesture and was happy. He started feeling very happy, as if all his desires were fulfilled.

Murali opened the lock up room, went inside, and obtained the signature on some papers.

" Move!" was the only word a little harsh and Venkata Swamy felt hurt. He kept staring at Amma. Amma sat on a mat and was looking very pathetic. The walls of the jail were failing to prevent her several thoughts.

"You are a girl and now got puberty. From now on you should not play and jump like boys. In fact, you should not mingle with the boys.

"With the words of her aunt Kotamma, Rajeswari became very silent and kept quiet without even venturing to reply.

"This happens every month. Do not worry about it and you will understand it in due course of time" her aunt pacified her.

"Come Rajeswari, Come and sit here!" her aunt called her and made her sit on a mat in the verandah.

Rajeswari did not understand anything. She simply obliged her aunt's instructions and sat on the mat. Four days went with fanfare.

Many relatives came to visit and all were delighted. Every lady told Rajeswari the same words as precautions to be taken again and again playing with her mind.

She got up early, finished her daily chores wore the uniform and organized her books in the bag and got ready to go to the school. Her aunt questioned Rajeswari where she was going and Rajeswari replied that she was going to the school.

"What? You are not a child anymore now. You cannot go to School and mingle with all boys. You have to remain at home and attend to household work till you get married"

"If I attain adulthood could I not go to the school?" Rajeswari put a question to herself.

"What is this? Why should I not continue my studies? Prasad, elder brother, is he not continuing his studies? Why can't I do the same thing? Is it a crime to be born as girl? "

Several thoughts surrounded young Rajeswari.

"I am always better than brother Prasad in studies in the School but I have to stop my studies just because I attained puberty. What is the reason for all such developments?"

She could not find any answer to all the doubts and questions that arose in her mind. Is it because of my aunt, who is looking after me or is there any other reason?

Even though Prasad got poor ranks in his class, he continues his studies uninterrupted. Aunt always praises and appreciates Prasad about his studies. She always presents new dresses to Prasad showing lots of affection. Talking about Rajeswari or thinking or planning about her, never happens. All the household work is to be done by Rajeswari only. Aunt never comes to her to enquire whether she took her food or how she felt etc. Aunt was looked upon like a beautiful demon to her. Aunt always talks to others about getting Rajeswwari married and sending her to the other family. If it is a monthly period, she would call it inauspicious and makes her sit on the mat outside for the three days. But there wouldn't be any rest for her. All those days also she has to get up very early in the morning, take a bath, sweep the entire place outside the house, remove the garbage wash all the utensils etc. By the time Sun rises she has to sit on the mat again. Even if she feels hungry, she can dine only once in the day time all the four days.

Who might have taught all these procedures to aunt so that she was abiding by all of them and follow them meticulously and sincerely? The days were supposed to be moving smoothly so to say. Food was given to Rajeswari only to survive. But is the food sufficient or not, only time can decide.

The four days every month was simply hell to Rajeswari. The body pains and the pains in the stomach uneven discharge of blood, inadequate food and heavy manual work are the gifts to the girl in her world.

Days months and years rolled down. There was not much change in her lifestyle. She did not even know about the words like existence of freedom or life freedom of speech and continues to live in such dark days.

When her aunt observed that Rajeswari attained the age for marriage she hurriedly got her married without weighing the pros and cons very fast. Raghu, her husband started the family life in the same place. Though he was well educated he never disobeyed his parents. Whatever was prescribed by his mother, he put it into practice immediately. Even in the time of monthly periods also he obeys his mother.

When she was at her aunt's house the whole of her household work was her duty. Now after the marriage services to her husband were added to the household work. If Raghu wants to take her out, he takes her out with a purely dictatorial and dominating attitude. She could never say no or refuse.

Her desires, pleasures, needed feelings are never recognized or considered by her husband or by her in laws. She was almost an inanimate article. Her husband satisfied all his physiological needs with her whether she liked it or not or even whether she feels comfortable or not. It is simply a hell for her. None was there to share her feelings or to express her discomfort. The dissatisfaction was getting piled up and testing her patience.

When Rajeswari became pregnant all the friends and relatives were invited for a function. They did not inspire any pleasure or happiness or comfort in her in spite of the celebration or festive activity.

When Rajeswari herself was suffering discrimination, her husband's sister Eswari was also found to be suffering with similar and more inconveniences. She was working as a software engineer and earning lakhs of rupees every month. Her husband was also a software engineer and was getting a salary of more than a lakh of rupees.

When Eswari became pregnant, she was made to take a long leave from her office. After her delivery to look after the child and the husband she had to resign from her lucrative job altogether.

Her family never felt sorry for her quitting the job with a hefty salary but preferred Eswari should not attend the office. Taking care of her child and satisfying her husband remains to be the prime duties of Eswari.

Vanajakshi poured kerosene on her body and ventured self-immolation being unable to bear the torture of her husband and the inhuman treatment of her in laws.

The flames engulfing her were still fresh in the memory of Rajeswari and were dancing before her eyes. She could never forget those incidents. People opine that ladies do have delicate hearts but in reality, unless one was very strong hearted, she cannot survive.

If the humiliating treatment shown by the husband and his family, the discriminating attitude by all and sundry, the hecklings from others were to be withstood one should muster enough courage. Else one has to think of sacrificing her life.

With the sound of lunch bell Rajeswari came out of her circle of thoughts and memories. She got up and joined the queue with her lunch plate. Though they were all woman prisoners everyone has to face the discrimination there also.

If one of them was good looking, she had to face a shameful situation with the nasty comments from the fellow prisoners.

She moved ahead with her empty plate to the food serving point.

"Extremely proud because of her top-class beauty, but cannot satisfy husband, became a street bitch and finally landed here!". The derogatory remarks accompanied the food. Such nasty remarks were never heard by her either from her husband or her aunt.

"It is the unfortunate life for the ladies in this world"

Pacifying herself she took *Sambar* in her plate and moved to a tree nearby. She sat there on a big stone and started taking a few morsels of food.

Her heart was burning with anger and apathy. Such unfortunate discriminated life was given by my parents and it cannot be my fault. Why such inhuman conditions were prescribed for a woman by the elders in this world? But even in this modern life why ladies were being harassed in this manner? Why should she undergo all such difficulty and unwarranted experiences? Is this because she was a female?

Are there not weaknesses for the man? Are they so powerful to control the nature? With every morsel of food, her thought process was changing from one aspect to another very fast.

Can there be any liberation from such discriminating world? When will it happen and how? Was it only an unfulfilled wish or was it a very greedy desire? Will it happen at least after her death?

The silence teaches some messages and pave way to some more thoughts. She finished her food with *Sambar* and went into her prescribed barrack and laid down there.

"Shanmugam ! Do you get what I told you? Do exactly that way. There should not be any deviation from the plan!"

"Yes. I follow your words!"

"Mani! What are you doing? Make a concrete and foolproof arrangement without any folly or any change!"

"Yes, I will do that way!"

"Siva is yet to come!"

"He is on the job!"

"Don't worry, Everything would be correctly done. You kindly take rest and be comfortable! "

"It is O.K! By dawn tomorrow, the work must be completed as planned. Please take necessary steps and complete it!"

Before sunrise agricultural workers while crossing the feeder canal in the field were shocked to find three dead bodies floating in the drain.

They went near the bodies, observed what happened there, and gave information to the police. The police came early and examined the bodies. They identified the male body as that of Raghu, the female body as that of Kotamma, and the child as Raghu's son.

Even after the enquiry, the reason for the deaths could not be detected by the police. Raghu''s wife Rajeswari was not seen in the house. Police were searching for her but in vain.

It was all bustling big with activity in Devaraya Samudra.

People were reaching there in large numbers with a fond hope that all their several wishes would be completely fulfilled in Amma's ashramam. Among those, there were several policemen too in the devotees. Without even asking or seeking, gold, gifts, cash, milk, ghee and several other articles, cashew, almonds and other costly dry fruits were pouring in from various devotees as offerings in the Ashramam. Within a very short period the place became a pilgrimage centre and was very popular.

Ashramam was flourishing with several new developments.

Amma was very happy. Her happiness knew no bounds because of the reverence shown by one and all to her. She was the queen of that small place. Without imposing any limits on the activities there. She felt very happy and wished her life should move on so fulfilled forever.

Since everything was going on very smoothly and softly Amma's Ashramam was flourishing day by day. Amma became Godess in human form to all those devotees whose wishes and desires were getting fulfilled.

Since Amma was getting quality food which was not available to her earlier, she turned out to be more and more beautiful with improvement in her color, and complexion.

Since many police were visiting the ashramam, it was all going on very peacefully without any law-and-order problem.

In the research and investigation of the police higher authorities, Rajeswari was identified as involved in the murder, cheating and other crimes. She was arrested and kept in the police custody.

When she was produced before the magistrate, she was ordered for 14 days' remand. The investigation and the legal process continued.

Rajeswari suddenly woke up from her sleep and looked to her left. Her son Akhilesh was sleeping there. She patted him affectionately.

She wanted to get down from her bed. Since the bed sheet was very thin her silver rings of her toes got entangled with the bed sheet and hence, she could not move down as expected. She brought her both the feet together and moved the bed sheet aside. She got down from the cot and looked at the feet of her husband Raghu who was fast asleep.

She was in a confused state whether it was a part of her dream or a sheer reality. She kept staring at her husband's feet respectfully and prayerfully!

*